Don't
Look Back

Especially for Girls® Presents

Don't Look Back

LEE WARDLAW

AN AVON FLARE BOOK

DON'T LOOK BACK is an original publication of Avon Books. This
work has never before appeared in book form.

AVON BOOKS
A division of
The Hearst Corporation
1350 Avenue of the Americas
New York, New York 10019

Copyright © 1993 by Lee Wardlaw Jaffurs
Published by arrangement with the author
Library of Congress Catalog Card Number: 93-90349
ISBN: 0-380-76419-9
RL: 5.5

First Avon Flare Printing: November 1993

AVON FLARE TRADEMARK REG. U.S. PAT. OFF. AND IN OTHER COUNTRIES,
MARCA REGISTRADA, HECHO EN U.S.A.

Printed in the U.S.A.

For Joan L. Oppenheimer,
who encouraged me to begin.
And to the survivors of Hurricane Iniki,
whose spirit leads Kauai toward a new beginning.

1

"Ladies and gentlemen, we're experiencing a little turbulence. Please take your seats and make sure your seat belts are securely fastened. Thank you."

The intercom switched off. Suddenly, the plane bounced, my heart started tap dancing, and what remained of my composure made an exit, stage left.

"Hey, Drew, you're not going to be *sick,* are you?"

I glanced at Kristin. Wouldn't you know it. Her first flight ever, and the only panic I saw in her face was caused by the thought that I might throw up in her lap. Life just isn't fair.

I unclenched my teeth long enough to whisper: "Not sick. Dying."

"What?!"

"I—I'm having an anxiety attack."

Kristin pushed a strand of blond hair behind one ear and stared at me, eyes wide with fascination. "Really? How do you know?"

"Heart's pounding . . . hair's sweating . . . can't breathe." I groped for the air-conditioning vent above my head and gave the nozzle a twist. The cold, dry air stung my wet forehead.

"Kris, I've got to get off this plane. Look out the window. Any sign of the islands yet?"

"Nope."

"You sure?"

"Yep. Just water. Miles and miles and *miles* of water. Look for yourself."

"No way!" I shut my eyes. Just glancing out that window would be enough to send my stomach into a plunging spiral. I hated that feeling. Hated teetering right on the edge of nothingness. One tiny step and I'd be falling, falling. Out of control. No way back. Nothing to grab onto except the overwhelming sensation of helplessness.

The plane lurched again. Kristin let out a whoop. "Just like a roller coaster! Oh—sorry. Those bother you too, don't they?"

I could only nod. My throat felt dry as an old popsicle stick.

Kristin squeezed my hand. "Why don't you try some of those relaxation exercises? Maybe they'll help."

I nodded again, my fists clenching each time the plane dipped. Kristin was right. I needed to concentrate on pleasant thoughts, calming thoughts. If only Mom had let a doctor hypnotize me before the flight.

"Honey, you're seventeen years old," she had said. "That's old enough to know that hypnosis only deals with symptoms, not your problems."

"But Mom, it's a five-hour flight. I can't survive that long. There's just no way!"

She smoothed my bangs. "You *can* do it, Drew. But I know you're scared. How about if I make an

2

appointment for you with a therapist? Maybe you should talk to a professional about this fear of heights."

"Never mind," I'd said. "I'll figure out something else." The last thing I wanted was some brain archaeologist digging around in my head, trying to find choice little artifacts like why I had nightmares about falling. Or why I kept Dad's letter wedged behind a secret flap in my wallet.

My stomach clenched as tightly as my fists. I shoved the mental image of that letter to a dark corner of my mind. Thinking about Dad now would only make matters worse.

I reclined my seat. Took a couple of slow, deep breaths. Then I began an exercise I had learned in a self-hypnosis book at the library. Slowly, the high whine of the jets and chatter of passengers grew distant, indistinct.

Touch your thumb to your index finger. As you do so, let your mind wander back to a time when your body felt healthy fatigue from an exhilarating physical activity.

We're hiking a steep trail in Yosemite—Mom, Dad, my brother Dillon, and I. I'm thirteen and hate my braces, my pointy nose, and hiking. Dillon's nine. He holds Dad's hand and trudges snail-like because of his asthma. He's been lucky this trip: no asthma attack all weekend. Mom brings up the rear. I'm surprised she's come along. Usually she avoids Dad's three-blister hikes.

"We'll never get to the top of this hill," I wail. Dad just gives me his slow smile and shakes his head. His dark curls dance in the breeze.

"Impatient, just like Mom," he says, throwing

3

her a teasing glance. "Always looking for short-cuts."

Mom returns the glance and says, panting, "A short cut . . . certainly would . . . make this hike a . . . whole lot easier!"

Frustrated, I kick a stone with the bulky toe of my hiking boot.

"C'mon, you guys," Dad coaxes. "Can't you appreciate the hike for its own sake? Smell the wildflowers, feel the earth under your feet."

"I think I'm going to appreciate this big rock for a minute," Mom says, easing herself onto it with a moan.

"Me too!" I flop down beside her.

"Me too," Dillon echoes.

Dad looks at the three of us with sad puppy-dog eyes. Mom laughs and tosses a dirt clod at him.

"Okay, okay," I say. "I give in. Race you, Dad!"

I leap up and speed on ahead, leaving Dad in my dust. At last I reach the crest of the hill. I'm tired, my breath coming in gasps. Dad jogs up behind me. I turn to ask *When are we going down again?*—and stop. Diamonds of sweat glisten in his beard. His cheeks are flushed and he's smiling. And I see the golden valley spreading below us in the expression of that smile.

"Look, Drew," Dad says. "There's the trail we climbed!"

I follow his gaze. The trail slithers and slides for what looks like miles, past patches of melting snow and brave-standing trees. Mom and Dillon look so small, sitting on their rock. They wave.

It's then I notice the muscles in my legs. They twitch and tingle and feel warm. My heart beats

4

friendly in my ears. I lick my lips and taste salt. It tastes good. And I *feel* good. Not just because I'm here, but because of what I had to do to get here.

"Beautiful, isn't it?" Dad says.

I answer by taking hold of his hand. We stand in silence, just the two of us, for a long time. Dad gazing down at the valley, I gazing up at the sunlight that touches his smile.

Touch your thumb to your middle finger. As you do so, let your mind wander back to the nicest compliment you have ever received.

It's only a month ago, my seventeenth birthday. I'm at Mom's art gallery in San Francisco, waiting for her to finish with a client so we can go out to celebrate. There's a new charcoal drawing hanging on the back wall. It's a nude, curled and sensuous like a cat. Her face has dainty, kittenish features.

"I wish *I* looked like that," I say wistfully, when the client leaves.

"Mmmmm." Mom puts her arms around me. "Yes, from an artist's point of view, she's lovely. But in real life? I'll bet hubby calls her 'Thunder Thighs.'"

I know she's teasing, trying to cheer me up. But it doesn't help.

"At least she *has* a figure," I say. "Mom, why am I so skinny? And why does my face have all these *angles?* The only round part of my body is an occasional zit."

Mom turns me to face her. Her intense gray eyes, which can rake over paintings with cold, appraising perfection, now look as blue and soft as her flowing silk blouse.

5

"Watch what you say, Drew Mueller. Remember, you're critiquing my finest work yet." With a finger Mom traces my nose, chin, and a tear that escapes down my cheek. "You have very striking features, hon. A lovely Grecian nose. Dark eyes and brows—curious, questioning. A determined-looking mouth. Yet those freckles keep you from seeming too serious. So do these." She plays with the wisps of hair that curl across my forehead. Even though I wear my long hair pulled back, these strands daily defy the large barrette.

A lump tugs at my throat. "You're talking like an artist, Mom. What about in real life?"

"Drew, art should always be *better* than real life. It should represent the best inside us, or the best we want to be. And that's you. You're very critical at times. Dissatisfied. But I can see in the proud way that you walk, the way you hold your head, that you're struggling to change. To learn. To grow. There's a—a *passion* inside that makes you very, very beautiful. You'll see it someday. I promise."

I hug her. We're the same height now, and her silver-blond hair brushes against my cheek. For some reason, I believe the things she's said. I don't know why. She's my mother, it's her job to admire her kid, isn't it? Yet I believe her. It's my birthday. And what Mom said is the best present I've ever received.

"Ladies and gentlemen, we'll be landing at the Honolulu International Airport in just a few moments. Please make sure your tray tables are locked, and bring your seats to their upright position. Thank you."

I opened my eyes. I had only finished two relaxation exercises, but I felt calmer. The turbulence had stopped, and Kristin was nudging me in the ribs.

"Aren't you *excited?*" She grinned, cocking her head in that half-pert, half-flirt gesture she was famous for.

I had to smile. And I wished, for about the thousandth time, that I was more like her. Kristin enjoys everything with great gusto: from strutting with the school band during football halftimes (believe it or not, she plays the drums!) to bawling her eyes out over a sentimental commercial. For Kris, around every bend lies Adventure! Mystery! Romance! Her entire life is one giant exclamation point. Lately, mine had become a question mark.

"Drew. Drew!"

Kristin's voice scattered my thoughts. She was facing the window, hands pressed against the wall as if to keep herself from leaping out.

"We're *landing!*" she squealed.

The plane banked and I moaned. My heart raced. Sure, I wanted to get down, but I had kind of hoped to do it while unconscious.

"Kristin," I managed to choke out. "Hold my hand."

She grabbed it without taking her gaze away from the window. "Don't look down," she ordered. "Now recite multiplication tables. Aloud."

I shut my eyes.

"Drew, I think we're flying over Pearl Harbor!"

"Two-times-two is four. Two-times-three is six . . ."

"Oh, the water is so blue. Almost turquoise. Look—surfers!"

"Two-times-nine is eighteen, two-times-ten is twenty . . ."

"I see Diamond Head, Drew. Just like on the postcards!"

"Two-times-twelve is twenty-four, two-times-thirteen is twenty-five . . ."

"Twenty-six," Kristin corrected.

"Whatever. Aren't we down yet?"

Bump. Thunk. Roar.

We'd landed. Don't know where the real brakes are in a 747, but with both feet planted against the seat in front of me, I'm sure I helped the pilot stop that plane.

"We're down, Drew."

I sighed and opened my eyes. Lilting Hawaiian music filled the cabin. We were still taxiing to the terminal, yet Kristin and half the other passengers had stood up, fumbling and grabbing for purses, bags, and children. Over the intercom, the flight attendant patiently urged everyone to sit down, but nobody paid any attention.

Kris slung her purse over one shoulder, whacked her head on the luggage bin, and rubbed the sore spot, unconcerned.

"You should be proud of yourself, Drew Mueller," she said. "Here, this is for you. For a flight well done!" She reached into her purse and pulled out a tiny plastic trophy. A gold paper plaque on the front read THE BEST.

I gave her a strong hug. "I did do it, didn't I? Thanks. This is—" I started to giggle "—this is probably the tackiest thing I've ever seen!"

Kristin laughed too. "Just think, only one more short flight to Kauai, and all your problems will be over!"

8

My chest tightened and I groaned.

"Hey, don't crack on me now." Kristin waggled a finger. "You're on a roll, kiddo. You survived one flight and you can survive the next. Really. The worst is over."

I sat back in my seat. "It's not that—" I began.

"Oh." Kristin bit her lip. "You mean, your dad."

"Yeah."

"But Drew, you'll get to see Dillon after two long years! And I'll be right beside you the whole time. You can hold my hand twenty-four hours a day, if you want. It'll be okay. You'll see."

"Sure. Thanks," I said, forcing a smile.

Yet Kristin's words didn't help. After all, she'd be going home in two weeks. Home to her mom and dad. Home to a normal family. I didn't have that choice. Mom was traveling across Europe. That's why I had to spend the summer with my father. A father I hadn't seen since he walked out of our house two years ago.

A father part of me wished I'd never see again.

2

Our interisland flight landed an hour later. I leaned over Kristin to peer out the window, anxious to catch a glimpse of Dillon. But would I even recognize him? With the exception of pictures, I hadn't seen him in almost two years.

At first, after the divorce, I had been shocked when Dillon decided to live with Dad in Hawaii, instead of with Mom and me. Then I felt hurt. Betrayed. But now, nothing mattered except seeing my baby brother again.

"I wonder if he still has asthma," I fussed, grabbing my carry-on and heading for the plane's exit. "I wonder if he's grown. I wonder if he's still cute—"

"I wonder if he has any cute *older* friends," Kris said.

We stepped out into the hot, tropical sun. A balmy gust of wind tugged at my hair and billowed Kristin's thin colorful skirt. The breeze smelled different from the cool salt-air of San Francisco. Heavier. More fragrant. A combination of ripe fruit, damp earth, fresh rains—and jet exhaust.

"Come on," Kristin urged. "Let's go!" She

flew down the stairs like a cascading waterfall. I followed more slowly, unable to take my eyes away from the dancing palm trees or the lush mountains poking their peaks into the intense blue sky. A balloon of excitement swelled inside me. I was in Hawaii! And only seconds away from seeing Dillon.

I spotted him immediately.

"Dillon!" I pushed past Kristin. My brother stood behind a chain-link gate, dressed in baggy, khaki-colored shorts and a bright yellow T-shirt. He looked taller. *Older.* I darted through the gate. We nearly collided in our hug.

"Aloha, Sis!" he said grinning. "Welcome." With a formal air he placed a pink-flowered lei over my head. Then he stumbled back, his cheeks flushed.

I grabbed him for another hug, not caring if he was embarrassed, not caring if I crushed my flowers.

"Wow, Dillon, you're so tan. You look like a native!" The yellow T-shirt accented the golden tone of his skin and the buttery highlights of his brown hair.

Dillon straightened at my compliment. "Thanks," he said. "Patsy says if I get any tanner, I'll look like a Menehune."

"What's a Menehune?"

"What's a Patsy?" Kristin asked, finally catching up. "Wooo, Dillon, cuter than ever! Hey, gorgeous, don't I get a lei, too?"

Dillon presented her with one made of white, sweet-smelling plumerias. He blushed when Kris gave him a loud kiss in return.

"Okay, where's the car?" Kristin continued. "I'm hot. I'm ready for a swim. I'm ready to *go!*"

"Don't you think we'd better find your luggage first?" asked a voice from behind us.

I turned. A tall, dark-haired man stood there. He smiled at me, a slow, quiet smile.

"Hi, Dr. Mueller!" Kristin said.

"Dad?" I hardly recognized him. His wild curls were cropped short against his head. And his beautiful beard! Gone. As a little girl I used to rub my nose in its fuzzy thickness, but now . . . "Dad, you *shaved.*"

He passed a hand down one cheek and under his chin, as if he'd forgotten. "About a year ago," he said.

We stood staring at each other, awkwardly, for a long minute. "It's good to see you, Drew," he said at last. "You too, Kristin." He stepped forward and put an arm around my shoulders. I caught a faint whiff of Dad-scent, a gentle mixture of soap and warm skin. Of home.

My heart tugged. For a second I wanted to bury my face in his shirt, breathing his safe, secure smell. Then I stiffened. This wasn't the old Dad. This dad had deserted Mom without warning, had taken Dillon away, had written that letter, hidden deep in my wallet. . . .

I pulled back, pretending to fumble with my bag.

"Well." He cleared his throat. "I'll bring the truck around. Back in a minute."

"Give me your claim checks," Dillon said. He ran off in search of our luggage, his thongs slapping against his heels.

Kristin and I waited at the front of the open-air terminal. She sat on the curb, legs outstretched, her skirt pulled up to her knees. Eyes closed, she

12

lifted her face to the hot sun in her Kristin Strategic Tanning Position.

"Ahhhh," she murmured. Then: "You didn't even hug him."

I shrugged. "So?"

"He's your *dad.*"

"That doesn't mean I have to like him, does it?"

Kristin opened her eyes and stared at me. "But, Drew, you guys used to be so close. I mean, I can understand why your parents split. They were so *different.* Your mom is a classy, city lady. And your dad is so outdoorsy. I used to think he was Paul Bunyan! But you and your dad really *liked* a lot of the same things. Remember how he used to take you out for a crab dinner once a week at Fisherman's Wharf? And how he always told those great ghost stories at the Girl Scout camp-outs?"

"Stop, Kris." A white panic had flared inside me. My voice quivered. "I can't talk about this now, okay?"

"But, Drew—"

"Please."

Kristin fell silent. I sat hugging my knees, waiting for the ripples of panic to ebb.

The silence between us stretched on. It seemed to eclipse the whine of another jet and the happy chatter of vacationers boarding a tour bus a few feet away.

"Don't be mad," Kristin said at last, touching my tennis shoe. "Or—I'll tie your feet together."

I looked down to catch her gleefully knotting my laces.

"Kris-tin!" I bonked her on the head with my purse, then leaned over to retie my shoes. "I'm

13

not mad, okay? Just tired and irritable and hot. Wish I hadn't worn these jeans." I pulled at the cotton shirt that clung damply between my shoulders. "Where's Dad with that car?"

A horn bee-beeped. Kristin and I got to our feet as a battered truck pulled beside the curb, engine sputtering. Huge patches of orange rust spread across its panels like overgrown weeds.

"Where'd Dad get this?" I said to Dillon as he stowed our suitcases in back. "What happened to the Mercedes?" Then I remembered. As part of the divorce settlement, Mom and Dad had split the money from the sale of the car, house, and medical practice.

Dillon shrugged. "I guess Dad can't afford anything else."

"What are you talking about?" I asked, astonished. "He got half of everything. And he's still a doctor, isn't he? Even working in a clinic, he should at least be able to afford a Honda."

Dillon shut the tailgate with a bang. "You can't put surfboards in a Honda."

I glanced at him in surprise. He sounded as if he were my *older* brother.

"All set?" Dad called out the window. "One of you girls will have to sit in back with Dillon. There's not much room up front."

"I will," Kristin volunteered.

"No, I will," I said. "Pretty grimy back here. And you've got a skirt on." Before she could argue, I clambered into the truck bed after Dillon. Kristin glanced at me, then nodded in sudden understanding.

"Great truck, Dr. Mueller!" she said, scooting into the passenger seat.

14

I gave a mental sigh. Good ol' Kris. I don't know what I would've said to Dad, being alone with him for the first time in two years. But Kris, she could make conversation with a soda cracker.

Within a few minutes we had driven through the city of Lihue. I felt disappointed, although I don't know what I'd been expecting. Maybe grass shacks and flaming tiki torches. But Lihue looked like any other small town. Gas stations, shopping centers, churches. I even caught a glimpse of the Golden Arches.

"McDonald's in paradise?" I asked.

Unconcerned, Dillon scratched a mosquito bite on his leg. "Just wait," he said.

We rumbled down a hill, then past a huge ramshackle building. An ancient smokestack towered over several rusty dinosaur-like cranes.

"Old sugar cane mill," Dillon shouted above the wind. The truck had picked up speed. We turned south, leaving the town and mill behind. A different world emerged. We flashed past acres and acres of sugar cane, standing in parade-perfection in the red-brown earth. Around one corner, I saw a tiny grotto of lush ferns and a waterfall. In the distance, cloud-pillows billowed white above mountains so densely covered with green they looked like rich velvet.

"Wait'll you see Poipu," Dillon said. "That's where we live. A couple blocks from one of the best bodysurfing beaches in the islands. Good surfing spots, too."

"Can you really surf?" I asked, amazed. "What about your asthma?"

Dillon shrugged. "Hasn't bothered me."

I couldn't believe it. All too vividly I remem-

15

bered those years of late nights when Dillon would wake up, panicked and wheezing. Mom would come into my room, her arms crossed against the cold, saying, "Drew, honey, you awake? Can you sit up with Dillon for a while? He's calling for you."

"I'm great on a boogie board," Dillon was boasting. "But Patsy's teaching me to surf, too. Jane took videos of me the other day. Says I look pretty awesome for a *haole*. That's a white person. You know, from the mainland." He glanced at me as if I'd taken offense. "She was just kidding about the *haole* part."

I poked one of his knobby knees. "Patsy and Jane. Are they your girlfriends? I'm jealous! Having a sister around this summer is sure gonna cramp your style."

Dillon frowned. "Jane isn't *my* girlfriend. She's Dad's. And Patsy is—"

"Wait a sec. Dad has a *girlfriend?*"

Dillon nodded. "Yeah. Didn't you know about Jane? He met her when he first moved here. She's been living with us since Christmas."

My throat felt tight. All those nights Mom had spent alone, wandering around our apartment, crying and clutching a soggy tissue. All that time Dad had been with a girlfriend!

Dillon must have seen the anger in my face. "Dad promised he'd write and tell you," he said. He plucked at a loose piece of rope, looking suddenly young. "He promised. Didn't he even tell Mom?"

I shook my head. "No, but you know how—" my voice caught "—how Dad loves surprises."

Dillon bent toward me, his eyes pleading. "Dad

16

has changed, Drew. You'll see. And you'll like Jane. Really. She's half-Japanese, half-Hawaiian. She knows the hula and all sorts of Hawaiian legends, and she's really funny."

Tears pricked my eyes. I turned my head, letting the cool wind blow my hair across my face so Dillon couldn't see. I wanted to ask if Jane had somehow caused our parents' break up. And if Dillon secretly hoped, like I did, that one day Mom and Dad would get back together. But I couldn't say a word. If I did, I knew I'd start to cry.

I tried to swallow my hurt. Again, I felt somehow betrayed. How could Dillon be so calm about Dad and another woman? How could he forget what Mom, what all of us, had been through?

I leaned back against the cab, eyes closed, and touched my thumb to my ring finger. Dillon's presence faded.

Let your mind wander to a time when you had a very special conversation with a family member or friend.

It's six months ago, right before Christmas. I work after school, three afternoons a week, as an office assistant for a small ad agency. I'm getting ready to leave one afternoon when I hear Jack grumbling. Jack is twenty-one, just out of college. He has a solemn mouth and deep green eyes. This is his first full-time job.

"Something's not right," he mumbles half to himself. He lays a mock-up on my desk as if it were a newborn baby. "Drew, I need an honest opinion. Look at this magazine ad. There's something wrong, but I don't know what."

The ad is for a new downtown hotel, The Majestic. TREAT YOURSELF ROYALLY, the ad says. Above the simple words is a picture of an elegant skyscraper. Its gold-glass windows glint brilliantly, like a crown in the sun.

"I see your problem," I say. "See we're looking at the hotel face-on. I think you should shoot your camera at an angle, from below the building, looking up. Like a peasant kneeling before a king. That'll make the hotel seem more, well, more majestic!"

Jack looks at me as if he's never seen me before. And then as if I'm some rare creature. "Grab your coat," he says. "Let's get some hot chocolate."

We sit by the window in a cozy coffee shop, watching rain splash the sidewalks. Sometimes I sense his green eyes watching me. Sometimes I glance at his lips and the way they dip down on one side when he smiles. But mostly we talk. And talk.

My heart feels warm. Warm as my hand, curled around the large mug of steaming chocolate. No one has ever listened or talked to me like this before. No one has ever asked about my job, my love of ads and commercials. Friends at school think commercials are tacky. My sociology teacher says they make us buy things we don't want or need. Even Mom, who recognizes the creative talent behind them, says, "Come on, Drew, admit it. Wouldn't you rather spend your life selling Van Goghs to connoisseurs, than Tender Liver Bits to cats?"

But not Jack. He's like me. He likes the energy, the urgency that ads stir inside us. The colors, the sounds that shake up our senses and make us act! go! buy! live!

18

"When you finish college," Jack says, "we should open our own ad agency. Don't laugh! We'd make a great team. We both have beauty *and* brains. Always a successful combination. Now what shall we call our agency? Drew and Jack's? Jack and Drew's? I know—you could change your name to Jill, and we'd be Jack and Jill's! Snappy. Easy to remember, don't you think?"

I laugh some more.

"I'm only partly kidding," he says. "You have a quick mind, Drew. It'd be fun to work together."

I nod, and after a while Jack's hand covers mine. I like the way my fingers tingle beneath his. He wants to see me again, he says. Could we go out to a movie sometime?

I lie. Tell him he's too old for me, that I have a boyfriend who wouldn't like it. I can see in the shrug of his shoulders that he doesn't believe me. But he smiles—that wonderful, crooked smile—and says all right.

After he leaves, I sit for a long time, staring at his empty mug. It wouldn't have worked out, I tell myself. Sure, I could've gone out with him once or twice, like I had with other guys. But why let it go beyond that? Why let myself care? Look what had happened to Mom. She thought Dad loved her, that their love would last forever. Then—poof!

I shake my head. No falling in love for me. It only leads to breaking up. Jagged edges. But not my conversation with Jack. I'd always have that, smooth and whole, like a circle. Complete and safe and saved, forever in my mind.

"Drew, there's Poipu! See?"

Dillon's voice brought me back to the present. I

19

opened my eyes to find we were riding through a tunnel of tall trees. Their boughs arched above us, like huge fingers, intertwined. We emerged into bright sunshine again. Ahead, the road dipped and I saw a strip of blue-green. The ocean. Poipu Beach.

"It's only four o'clock," Dillon said. "We'll go for a swim, first thing."

I nodded. Anything to avoid facing Dad. And Jane.

"She's really all right," Dillon said, as if guessing my thoughts. "We have fun."

"Don't you miss Mom?" I blurted.

"Sure. But we talk a lot on the phone, you know that. And I'll be coming to see you guys at Christmas this year." He shrugged and looked away. "I like it here."

"Dillon," I said slowly, "do you like Jane better than Mom?"

He seemed to turn that over in his mind, like tasting a new kind of food. Why didn't he just say *no* right away?

"No," he said at last. "I like her different, if you know what I mean. Look, just give her a chance, okay?"

I forced a smile. "Sure, Dill Pickle." His nose wrinkled at the hated nickname, but I noticed the tug of a smile on his lips. Then his shoulders tensed.

"If you and Jane don't get along, you won't go anywhere, will you?" he asked.

"What do you mean?"

Dillon shrugged. "I don't know. You wouldn't go home with Kristin for the rest of the summer, would you?"

20

My heart softened. "No way. I just suffered through three thousand miles of heart attacks and you think I'm gonna get back on another plane?" I gave him a playful kick. "Uh-uh. Besides, you're going to teach me to bodysurf, aren't you?"

"Sure!" Dillon's shoulders relaxed and I thought I heard him sigh.

I turned and watched the strip of blue-green ocean grow wider, like a canyon yawning.

I won't leave, little brother, I wanted to say. *I'm only here because of you.* But I knew he wouldn't understand. Dillon had chosen to live here, so he couldn't possibly be as angry at Dad as I was. How had he gotten over it?

And Jane. How could Dillon talk about her so easily? After all those years living with Mom and Dad, how could he stand to watch Dad and another woman together?

No, Dillon wouldn't understand how much I was dreading this summer. And now, how much I dreaded meeting Jane.

3

"This is it!" Dillon sang out. The truck bounced over the ruts of a dirt-and-grass driveway, parking beside a small cottage. Balancing one hand on the tailgate, Dillon leapt out of the truck like a gymnast. "Don't forget to leave your shoes on the lanai," he said, grabbing our suitcases.

"On the what?" I asked.

Arms full, Dillon motioned with his head. "On the patio. Come on, I'll give you a tour." He skirted past a blooming hibiscus bush that nestled against the house. Kicking off his thongs, he pushed open a sliding screen door and scurried inside.

"He moves like a squirrel stuck in overdrive," I murmured to Kristin.

She laughed, then said, her voice awed, "Oh, Dr. Mueller, this is beautiful!"

Dad had followed me up the grassy path to the slate patio, but Kristin meandered about, first scooping up plumeria blossoms that lay strewn across the grass, then sprawling on a lounge chair. "I could stay here forever," she continued dreamily. "That view is to *die* for!"

I had to agree. The house rested on the gentle

slope of a hill that overlooked a valley filled with two-story condos. Surrounding them were palm trees, tennis courts, swimming pools, and a seemingly endless expanse of green lawn. Below that, to the right, I could see a strip of golden beach. To the left, the ocean splashed high against jagged lava rocks in a froth of turquoise and white.

"We like it," Dad said simply. "Five-minute walk to the beach, incredible sunsets—" His usual laid-back tone warmed with pride. "Plus, we've got two papaya trees, coconuts, and bananas. It's a bit noisy this time of year, though. That's a resort, below us." He pointed to the condos. "Most places up here are vacation rentals. We're renting, too. But I've bought an acre of land, back in the hills. We'll start building a home soon."

"A home for you and Dillon?" I asked casually. "Or for you and Jane?"

A split-second pause.

"A home for all of us," Dad said. Then: "I guess Dillon told you about her."

"Somebody had to," I whispered.

Dad heard me. His eyes widened, and a thorny silence pricked between us. What was he thinking? Had my words hit home? Was he angry? Hurt? There seemed little point in wondering. He'd never let me know.

"Your father had an unusual childhood, Drew," Mom had reminded me a few months ago. "His father, your Grandpa Joe, was a naval officer. Very strict. No nonsense. He raised your dad to believe it wasn't manly to show emotion, ever." She gazed through me, as if looking into the past. "Your dad couldn't cheer at football games. He couldn't hold my hand in public. He couldn't even cry at Grandpa

23

Joe's funeral. And then, all those years we were married—" Tears had welled in Mom's eyes. "I knew something was wrong. I could tell he was unhappy. But I couldn't get him to admit it, to talk about it. He'd just smile and say everything was fine, just fine. And then the way he left me . . . left *us*. Such a cold thing to do. Almost as if after a childhood of curbing emotions, he'd lost all capacity to feel . . ."

"Who's Jane?" Kristin asked, disrupting my thoughts.

I held my breath, waiting for Dad to say the words *She's my girlfriend*. I wanted to stand up to those words, stand up to Dad, be like him, cold and unfeeling. I could handle it. I wouldn't get mad. Anger showed you were hurt, and hurt showed you cared.

"Come on, you guys," Dillon called from inside.

"Coming!" I slid open the door.

"Shoes!" Dillon shouted.

"Oops." I about-faced, running into a barefooted Kristin. She clicked her tongue, grinning, and went inside. Kicking off my shoes, I could sense Dad watching me. My cheeks felt hot. But he chuckled as if the tension of the moment before had never existed.

"Dillon's obsessed with keeping the floor clean this week because it's his turn to sweep," he explained. "Just wait till it's your job. He'll track in enough mud and sand to start another island."

"Oh." I didn't know what else to say, what else to do. I just stood there, uncomfortable, waiting for him to finish talking.

"Jane and I often work odd hours at the clinic,"

24

he continued. "Some early evenings, an occasional weekend—so we all share chores around here. You'll have some, too, like cooking dinner, gardening, making the beds. I hope you don't mind."

"No," I said, giving him a fixed look. *"I* don't have a problem with responsibility."

An expression of, what?—pain? guilt?—flashed in Dad's eyes. I looked away, itching with shame, Mom's voice echoing in my ears.

"Try to curb that tongue of yours," she had said before I left. "It's grown sharper in the last two years, and if you use it, the only person you'll hurt is Dillon."

"Dillon? How—?"

"I know you don't want to see your dad, and I don't blame you. But until you're eighteen, he has every right to see *you.* So does Dillon. Your brother misses and loves you terribly. He also loves your dad. And if you're not careful, you'll say things that will force Dillon to choose between the two of you. Don't tear him apart like that, Drew. Please. Please take care in what you say. . . ."

I glanced through the screen door, hoping Dillon hadn't overheard. When I glanced back, Dad still had that unnamed expression in his eyes. His tone, though, was calm as ever.

"Well, I'm glad your mother is raising you so well," he said. "And at her request, I've arranged a part-time job for you. She said you were upset about having to leave the ad agency." He looked at his watch. "I've got to go to Koloa and get groceries for dinner. It's my night to cook. I'll fill you in on the job details this evening, all right?"

"Sure, okay." Working would keep me away

from the house. And if my job was with an ad agency . . . ! My heart soared. Maybe I'd be writing ads for Hawaiian stuff. Suntan lotions, hula lessons. PUT A LITTLE FIRE IN YOUR LIFE WITH VICK'S VOLCANO TOURS. YOU'LL LAVA IT!

I smothered a giggle and hurried into the house. "Dillon? Kristin?"

"Back here."

I followed their voices, first checking out the living room. A white, rattan couch and three chairs, padded with cushions of cool green-and-blue prints, were arranged cozily in the center of the room, facing the wide windows. There was also a glass coffee table, covered with stacked magazines. An old television squatted in one corner. In another, a dining table with four chairs sat on a round straw mat that spread across the tiled floor like a giant doily. The house had a faint musty smell.

"Here's my room." Dillon's head poked out of a door. "Actually, it's yours for the summer. I'm gonna sleep on the back porch. It's screened in and has a day-bed. The kitchen's over there, bathroom's down the hall. And that's Dad and Jane's room."

I peeked in, expecting a Japanese futon or a big-bellied stone Buddha. Instead, I saw a water bed with a scattering of pillows and two stuffed animals.

How old was Jane? I wondered. Forty going on nine?

Kristin tugged at my arm. "Hey, you can be nosy later. Dillon's taking us to the beach." She led me to our room, where we rummaged through

26

suitcases. "Ta-daaa!" she cried, when she had finished changing into a slinky copper-colored bikini. "Ready?"

"Not quite."

"What do you need? Suntan lotion? Towel?"

I glanced from my body to Kristin's and back again. "No. Major renovations." As a going-away gift, Mom had bought me a flowered one-piece. Pretty, but the high french-cut made my skinny legs look like paper-towel tubes. And as always, the top poofed out where I didn't. "At least if we go shell collecting," I added, plucking at the bra, "I know where I can store them."

"You're terrible!" Kristin threw my T-shirt at me. "Here, put this on and let's go."

Dillon was waiting for us outside. He had a boogie board under one arm, three towels under the other, and a pair of swim flippers tied to a rope thrown over his shoulder. "Brennecke's, here we come!" he cried.

We started down the hill. "What's Brennecke's?" I asked. "I thought we were going to Poipu."

"This whole area is called Poipu," Dillon explained. "And there *is* a Poipu Beach, but it's a cove. Brennecke Beach is where the surf is. Wow, look at that wave!"

We were close enough to see the beach more clearly. Dozens of heads bobbed in the blue-green water, waiting. Then, as the wave swelled higher, arms seemed to grow out of the heads, windmilling the bodies toward shore. Someone shouted "Wooooo!" as the wave started to fold. I caught my breath. Most people skimmed perfectly, at an angle, down the face of the wave. But others were

27

swept under in a thunderous crash of water and foam. I saw flailing arms and legs and a boogie board shooting straight into the air. Then the water raced back and heads surfaced again, to bob and wait for the next wave.

I froze in my tracks. "Geez, Dillon, that's supposed to be *fun?*" Even Kristin's face lacked its usual gung-ho expression.

"Well, it is easier with flippers," Dillon admitted. "But once you get out past where the waves break it's not so bad. I'll teach you, don't worry."

How could I not worry? I'm a strong swimmer—in a backyard pool with a plastic raft to float on. I'd only swum in the ocean once or twice. San Francisco rarely gets warm enough for swimming, and surfers with walruslike wet suits are the only ones who venture into the fifty-degree water.

We reached Brennecke's a few minutes later. The beach was crowded, but we found a place to spread our towels under the narrow shade of a lava retaining wall. Kristin and I stretched out, but Dillon stood, shifting anxiously in the sand.

"Uh, I'll see you guys later, okay?" he said.

I squinted up at him. "Where ya goin'?" Then I noticed a group of kids about Dillon's age sitting a few yards away. All were so tan their skin was the color of chocolate milk. One had sun-fried hair, the top layer the color of an egg yolk. "Hey, brah," he called.

"Howzit," Dillon answered. Without a backward glance, he strolled over to the group.

"Oh-oh," I said to Kristin. "There goes our bodysurfing instructor." *And* my baby brother. I couldn't believe he was embarrassed to be seen with me. What had happened to the days when he

28

would've dragged me by the hair to meet his friends?

"It doesn't look too hard," Kristin said in her ever-ready-to-try voice.

"I don't know." I watched the next wave roar in. Tourists stood close to shore, knee-deep and awkward in the rough foam. They squealed and giggled when the tide rushed back, yanking them off their feet. Only the locals seemed to be out where the action was.

"Let's at least get our feet wet," Kristin urged. "Maybe we can swim out in between sets."

My stomach did a backflip. "But the waves just keep *coming.*"

"Excuse me," a male voice said.

I turned, coming face-to-face with my own reflection. Then I realized I was staring into a pair of mirrored sunglasses that rested on the bridge of a sun-peeled nose. The guy wearing them squatted in the sand. He looked a little older than me and had tanned, broad shoulders. White rings of dried salt dotted across them.

"Can I help you?" I sounded formal, but my heart pounded. He looked like a guy in an ad I'd seen once for a pair of hundred-dollar sunglasses. Only in this case, you wouldn't want the glasses. Just the guy, at any price.

"I wasn't trying to listen in or anything," Sunglasses said, "but are you two from the mainland?"

Kristin gave her pert-flirt smile. "What gave you your first clue?"

Must've been me. No wonder he needed those glasses—to ward off the glare of my white body.

"I heard you talking," the guy said. "Listen, if

29

you've never bodysurfed before, you'll be better off at Poipu Beach Park. It's just a couple of blocks down the road.'' He smiled. ''They don't call Brennecke's 'Break Neck Beach' for nothing.''

''Poipu sounds good to me,'' I said, and stood up. When I leaned over to shake my towel, I glanced sideways at Kristin and caught a brief frown. Obviously, love at first drool. She wanted to stay. Not me. Within an hour, she and Sunglasses would be chatting and laughing, their foreheads almost touching. The only intimate interlude I'd have would be with a raging case of sunburn.

''Well, thanks for the advice,'' Kristin said. She gave him a dazzling smile. ''See you later.''

''Sure.'' The guy sauntered toward the water. With the sun shining sweet and warm on his hair, it looked the color of melted brown sugar. I wanted to touch it. Instead, I turned away.

''Pick up your towel and your tongue and let's go,'' I said.

Kristin didn't move. ''Isn't he *gorgeous?*'' she whispered. ''I just wish I could've seen his eyes. I hate those reflecting sunglasses. You never know who—or what—watches from behind the frames.''

''That's why I like them,'' I said. ''You can imagine a guy is almost anything. Mysterious, brilliant, dashing. Until he takes them off. Then I'm always disappointed.''

''Maybe that guy's different,'' Kristin argued.

I gave my towel a determined shake. ''Ha. Did you see his tan? No one gets that dark unless he's a surf rat or a loser. Probably dropped out of high school. Never worked a day in his life. And I'll bet he's a pothead.''

30

"He's not the only one." Kristin tugged at my arm. "Look."

I followed her gaze to where Dillon huddled with his friends. In disbelief, I watched as my brother took something from Mr. Yolk-hair. He put it to his lips and held it there for a long time. Then he laughed and blew smoke out.

I was stunned. Not Dillon! Then I saw Sunglasses approach Dillon's group. He squatted next to my brother and put his arm around his shoulder. He took the joint from Dillon's fingers. The sickening-sweet smell of grass mingled with the salt air.

"I guess you were right," Kristin said, regret filling her voice.

I felt empty with disappointment and anger. This was all Dad's fault. He never should've brought Dillon to Hawaii. Never should've taken him away from Mom and me. Dillon had always been a sweet kid, a smart kid. But now—

"Come on, Kristin," I said. "Let's get out of here."

4

"So what are you going to do?" Kristin asked as we walked to Poipu Beach. "Rat on your own brother? Not too cool."

"Neither's smoking pot. It's dumb. And Dillon knows better. Especially with his asthma." We walked in silence for a few minutes. "No," I said at last, "I'm not gonna rat on him. We're buddies. I'll talk to him myself. Tonight."

We reached the park. I thudded onto the edge of a picnic bench and gazed out at the water. "Dad never should've brought Dillon here. In San Francisco he went to a good school, had good friends. . . ."

"But I thought it was Dillon's decision to leave California."

I sighed. "Yeah, it was. But Mom never should-'ve left the choice up to him. I mean, what kid isn't going to jump at the chance to live in Hawaii?"

Kristin joined me on the bench. "You didn't," she said.

"Yeah, well." I shrugged, but my voice sounded ragged.

"Drew, um . . . I know this is a touchy subject, but do you want to talk? About your parents' divorce, I mean. I don't want to pry, but we're best friends. We've always been able to talk to each other about everything. Except this."

It was true. Kristin and I had been practically joined at the hip since birth. No topic was too sad, too embarrassing, too personal to discuss. At least, until Mom and Dad split up. I'd been putting Kris off for almost two years, saying, "It happened. It's over. I don't want to talk about it."

A catamaran skimmed across the horizon. Its white sails blurred for a second and I blinked back tears.

"Did they fight a lot toward the end?" Kristin coaxed. "Did they see a marriage counselor or anything?"

"No."

"Well, what exactly made them decide to split up?"

"They didn't decide anything. Dad decided."

"Oh." A pause. "Well, what did he say, Drew? What were his reasons?"

My thoughts slipped back to the first time Dad had called, two months after he left. I stood in the doorway of Mom's office, eavesdropping on her end of the conversation.

"Please tell me, Marc. What have I done?" she had said, her voice clotted with tears. *"What did I do that was so horrible that you had to leave? That you couldn't even say good-bye? . . . I know I promised, but damn it, my world is crumbling here! . . . Talk to me! Just for once, can't you please just . . . don't hang up. Marc! No, don't hang up! . . ."*

33

"Drew?" Kristin was peering into my face.

I brushed at my eyes. "Can we talk about this later, Kris? It—it's hard for me. Sometimes I can't even talk about it inside myself. Thanks anyway, though."

"Hey, sure. Just remember, if you ever change your mind, I'll be here."

"I'll remember."

Kristin leapt up and began an exaggerated belly dance. "I'll be here, here, here," she chanted in a nasal tone. Her arms slithered across her face, then above her head, fingers waving like tentacles. "Here with rings on my fingers and bells on my toes and a bone through my nose, ho ho!"

"Don't mind her," I said, confiding to an imaginary companion. "An escapee from Sunny Brook Mental Home. Terminal Weirdness, you know."

Kris dropped her arms. "True. And the only cure is lots and lots of salt water. Come on, race you!"

We ran. I won. The warm water lapped around me as I floated lazily on my back, the tension of airplanes and fathers being tugged away with the gentle ebb of the tide.

Sunglasses had been right about Poipu Beach. Calm. Peaceful. An arm of lava rock cradled the crescent-shaped cove in a natural seabreak. Tiny waves no higher than my calves tripped against the shore with soft swooshing noises. The water was so clear I could see the coarse gold sand below. When I stood up, a school of tiny, translucent fish zigzagged past my feet. I glanced at Kristin and grinned.

"Hey, it's getting late," she said after we'd been swimming for an hour. The sun, though still warm, was sinking lower in the sky. A few stragglers played volleyball in a sand court near the picnic area, but the beach was deserted.

"We'd better hurry," I said, heading for shore. We toweled off, then began the walk back to the beach house. Passing Brennecke's, I saw Mr. Yolk-hair sitting with a couple of girls. Sunglasses and Dillon were gone.

When we reached the house, I noticed a white Subaru station wagon cozily parked next to Dad's truck. Must be Jane's. Dillon stood nearby on the lawn, hosing the sand off his boogie board.

"Howzit, Sis. Poipu's cool, huh?" He grinned at me, his eyes red-rimmed and sleepy-looking.

"Yeah, it's great," I said. "Hey, Dillon, listen." I shot a glance at Kristin. She took the hose and moved a casual distance away, acting intent on spraying her feet. "Dillon, could we talk? It's important."

He looked at me. "Sure. After dinner, okay? Dad's barbecuing beef kabobs. They'll be ready in about twenty minutes. I want to grab a quick shower." He turned to scamper away, his cheeks coloring a bit. Did he know that I knew?

"Don't forget!" I called after him. "You coming, Kris?"

"In a bit. I want to watch the sunset."

I padded barefoot through the house. It felt good to have a few minutes alone. I needed to plan what to say to Dillon.

I opened the door of my room.

"Oh, hello! You're Drew, aren't you?"

I froze. A petite woman with dark, short-tousled hair stood near the bed with a pillow in her hand. She moved toward me, smiling, the other hand

35

outstretched. I shook it stiffly. Her fingers felt small yet firm against mine.

"I'm Jane Takahara, and I'm so glad you're here. Your dad and I have been looking forward to this visit for weeks." She motioned toward the bed. "Just changing the sheets. I knew Dillon would forget. Here, tuck in the other end of this blanket— though I doubt you'll need it tonight. It stays so warm here in the evenings. But, just to be on the safe side . . ."

I began to help with the bed. My movements felt mechanical, automatic, as if someone else were in control of them.

I'd pictured Jane differently. Tall and sexy in an elegant sort of way, like Mom, only with stereo-typed Oriental features: glossy blue-black hair streaming down to her waist, a Mona Lisa smile, and maybe a name like Sweet Leilani. Far from it. Wearing shorts, T-shirt, and aerobic tennis shoes, Jane looked toned and ready for a serious match of tennis.

"Great. Thanks for helping," Jane was saying. She gave me another warm, open smile, her gaze searching mine.

I felt awkward. Didn't know what to say.

"Uh, you're welcome, ma'am," I finally man-aged.

Jane's eyes widened. *"Please,"* she laughed, "could you call me Jane? I'm only thirty-six, much too young to be a ma'am." She slipped a case over each pillow, then gave one an enthusiastic whack. "You know, Drew, I had a whole speech prepared for you and everything, but now—" She sat on the bed with a sigh. "I'm just nervous, that's all. Me! And I've been a therapist for ten years!"

36

"Therapist?" I said. "You mean like a psychologist?"

Jane nodded.

Oh, no. She was probably analyzing every move I made, every word I didn't say. I turned and unlocked my suitcase with trembling hands.

A short silence. A dove gave a throaty coo outside my window.

"Drew—" Jane began. Another silence, as if she were choosing her words with care. "I wanted to say things like 'Welcome. I hope we'll be friends.' But all that sounds so corny, doesn't it? This is a difficult situation. I know you don't really want to be here. I know it was your mom's idea, not yours, for you to come—especially when she couldn't afford to take you to Europe. But *we're* glad you're here—all three of us. I mean that. And, well, I hope you'll let me know if there's ever anything you need."

I nodded, unable to trust my voice. It bothered me that she knew how I felt about coming here. How did she find out? Not from Mom. Maybe Dad had told her about this afternoon. My words and actions must have shouted my feelings loud and clear.

I took a pair of underwear from my suitcase, toying with a loose strand of elastic on the waistband. My hands still trembled. I didn't turn around.

The smile returned to Jane's lips. I could hear it in her enthusiasm. "Your dad mentioned you work at an ad agency. Sounds fascinating! And such an unusual job for a person your age. I'd love to know more about it. And if you have any questions about the islands, our life here, whatever, please, just ask. Anything."

37

I knew suddenly that there *was* something. *Sorry, Dillon,* I thought. *I promised to give Jane a chance, but I have to ask.*

"I just want to know one thing."

"Shoot."

I turned to face her, my stomach a tight fist. "Are you—are you the reason my Dad left us?"

Jane's face paled beneath her tan. "Whew," she said. "That certainly was blunt."

"I'm—I'm sorry," I mumbled. "I shouldn't have asked—"

"No, don't apologize. I did say you could ask anything, didn't I? And I suppose it's a reasonable question, especially if your dad never—"

Jane paused, gazing past me. When she glanced back, the color had returned to her face, but her voice had grown sad.

"The answer is no, Drew. Definitely no. Didn't you and your dad ever talk? No, I guess not. That's not his style, is it? Well, I'm working on that."

She shook her head. "I met your dad about six months after he left San Francisco. He'd just moved here from Honolulu. We met at the clinic. We started dating casually, and then things just . . . happened. I love him very much." She lifted a hand in a questioning gesture. "Um, is there anything else you want to know?"

"No, I guess not." I met Jane's level gaze. "Thank you."

She nodded, not smiling this time, as if to show she understood exactly how important and difficult my question, and her answer, had been to me. Before we had a chance to say anything else, someone thunked on the bedroom door.

"Dinner!" Dillon called. Another thunk.

38

"Drew, you decent in there? Kris wants you to bring her a dry T-shirt."

"That's our formal dinner attire around here," Jane said, as she headed out the door. "You'd better grab one for yourself, too. That damp bathing suit is going to feel pretty chilly when the sun goes down."

After she'd gone, I changed, hanging my bathing suit to dry on the sill of the open window. My stomach had unclenched a little. Part of me was glad Jane hadn't caused my parents' divorce, because I had to admit, begrudgingly, that I kind of liked her. Or at least, I liked her honesty. But another part of me was disappointed. It would've been easier to have someone to blame. To be able to say Dad left because Jane had cast a magical spell on him. But she hadn't. And that left me wondering. What made him leave the way he did?

I chose a T-shirt for Kristin, then wandered outside, following the chatter of voices. Kris and Jane sat beside each other at an umbrellaed table on the lanai, laughing and gabbing as if they were long-lost sisters. Dillon was helping Dad serve the sizzling beef kabobs, placing two atop a bed of rice on each plate. The air smelled of charcoal smoke and sweet teriyaki sauce. I scooted next to Kristin, handing her the shirt.

"Have you told Drew about her job yet, Marc?" Jane asked Dad.

He joined her at the table, taking the bowl of salad she handed him. "Only that she has one," he said.

"You're so lucky," Dillon broke in, barely understandable with his mouth stuffed with food. He swallowed vigorously and continued, "You'll be working with Patsy, my surfing instructor. And you'll get to be on the beach all day."

The excitement I'd felt earlier about the job faded. I put down my fork. "Something tells me I won't be working at an ad agency."

"I doubt there's even one on the island," Dad said. "No, you'll be working at the beach shack, up at Kapakai Plantation. It's a resort. You'll hand out towels to guests, rent snorkeling and swimming equipment, and make appointments for the surf lessons. Four dollars an hour, nine to noon."

"I was making five dollars an hour at the agency," I said.

"Here, it's a miracle you even have a job," Dad remarked. "A lot of locals are out of work, and college students flock to the islands during the summer, taking most of the evening waitress and bartender jobs, so they can beach it during the day."

"Sounds fun," Kristin said. "Think of all the gorgeous bartenders you'll meet!"

"It isn't exactly stimulating work, Marc," Jane said. She flashed me a sympathetic look. "Maybe we could find something else for you at the clinic. Or would you rather take the summer off? A real vacation wouldn't hurt."

"I already checked around. And there's nothing at the clinic," Dad said. "Besides, she and her mother are much alike. They love to work."

Her mother. The words made me feel cold. How could he call Mom that? How could he have loved her, married her, shared a home with her for all those years, and now suddenly talk about her as if she were a total stranger?

My throat ached. For what seemed the hundredth time that day, tears pricked my eyes. No, I couldn't cry. I *wouldn't* cry.

I pushed back my plate. "Could I be excused, please? I'm not very hungry."

Without waiting for an answer, I escaped into the house, back to my room. I didn't turn on the light. Just lay down on the bed, letting the darkening shadows pad around me, like soft cotton.

Someone knocked on the door. "Drew, could I talk to you?"

Dad. I sat up. "Sure. I guess so."

He came in and leaned against the door frame, as if needing it for support.

"I'm sorry about the job," he said. "There really isn't much available on the island, but if you'd rather not work there—"

"No. The job's all right. Really. I—I appreciate you getting it for me."

"Something's bothering you, though." A pause. "Do you . . . do you want to tell me what it is?"

Part of me wanted to shout, *It's you!* But the thought gave me that sickening, falling sensation in the pit of my stomach. I shut my eyes.

"Are things okay . . . at home?" Dad sounded tentative, as if he were blindfolded and had to make his way through a cluttered room. "I mean, with school. And work."

"School and work are fine," I answered.

"And your mother? Are you two getting on okay alone? When I call, you never say very much. And I wonder sometimes, you know, how you're doing."

My head jerked up. "I'm fine. Dillon's the one who's not okay." My words tumbled out, uncontrolled, like a desperate diversion.

41

"What are you talking about?"

"Kristin and I saw Dillon smoking pot today on the beach. Is that the kind of life-style he's picking up here in your paradise?"

Dad sighed and was silent.

"I've been afraid he'd experiment," he said at last. "Pot is so easy to get in the islands. But I trusted him. We had a deal. I'd told him as long as he was living with me, he wasn't to use any of that stuff." Dad ran a hand through his short-cropped hair. "I'm glad you told me. I'll take care of it."

He turned to go.

"What are you going to do?" I asked.

"That's between Dillon and me. I said I'd take care of it, didn't I?"

"How, Dad? *How* will you take care of it? By writing him a letter?"

Dad faced me again. His eyes held their usual calm, serene look. But his mouth was pinched at the corners.

We stared at each other for a long moment, before I finally looked away.

"I'll take care of it," Dad repeated. He shut the door softly behind him.

5

I hated myself. I was a rat. A slug. A wolf in sister's clothing. How could I have blurted that stuff about Dillon?

I flounced onto my stomach, hugging the pillow to my chest. What was Dad going to do? Worse yet, what would Dillon do? I could handle anything except the look in his eyes when he'd ask me: Why?

I got off the bed and began to unpack. Voices and occasional laughter drifted like gray smoke through the open window. Everyone was still eating. I decided to take a quick shower, then talk to Dillon before Dad did.

I grabbed my shampoo and robe, and headed for the bathroom.

The water felt good. I turned up the pressure, letting the hot spray rain hard on my head. It felt like it was melting the salty-stiffness of my hair. I wished it could melt the stiffness inside me. Rinse away the guilt, the anger, then send both spiraling down the drain.

I shut my eyes and touched my thumb to my pinky to do another relaxation exercise. Maybe it would help.

43

Think of the most beautiful place you've ever been. Now rest there for a while.

I'm seven years old. I awake one night. It's late. I know because the city is quiet with the faraway sounds of cars and a now-and-then siren. But a sliver of yellow light from the living room still shines under my closed bedroom door. I hear voices. Mama sounds the same as always: sure and right. But Daddy, he's not as quiet. There's a bubbling in his voice, like he'll never give up.

". . . price is right, Marlene," he's saying. "Ten acres of land, and a charming Victorian house, overlooking our own vineyard."

"Sounds lovely, Marc," Mama says. "But my gallery just opened. I'll need to work late for the first year or two, and with over an hour's commute to and from San Francisco—" She pauses. "Honey, when will I have time for you, the kids, work, a house, and a *farm?*"

"Let's try it for a year, Marlene. That's all I ask. One year, and if it doesn't work out, we'll move back to the city. All right?"

We move to Santa Rosa a couple of months later. I miss the city. The park. The bridge. But our house has banisters to slide down, and Daddy builds me a tree fort, and sometimes, in the mornings, I hear cows mooing in the distance.

The year slips by fast and quiet, like the water in our creek out back. Mama goes quietly to the city every day. Her eyes look tired, but Daddy's don't. He hums and jingles his keys each morning when he leaves for work.

The best day of that year is the worst day, too.

We're outside. Mama's sitting in a big wicker

44

chair, with Dillon on her lap. They're painting a picture together. Dillon giggles now and then. Daddy and I are rocking in the big hammock, between two shady oak trees. We're watching the sun go down. The sun looks bigger here than it did in the city. It looks like a huge circle of orange felt pressed against my teacher's flannel board.

"Watch, Drew," Daddy says, hugging me closer. "Watch how the sun makes the hills look like grape juice."

I hold my breath. As the sun sinks lower, the flat land and tiny hills around us turn a cool, liquid purple. Then the sun disappears, and I almost hear it sigh.

But it's really Mama. She shifts Dillon on her lap and says, "It's not working out, Marc."

"I know." A purple silence. "It's a good place to think though, isn't it?"

Mama nods. "But I need to think on my feet."

Daddy nods then, too. He gives me another hug. We hold each other a long time, rocking, rocking, and watching the sky melt dark.

"Watch for the moon, Drew," he says, but instead I bury my face in his shirt. Something's different. Daddy's voice doesn't bubble anymore, and I know that he's given up.

We move back to the city a few weeks later. . . .

"Hey! How long you gonna be in there?" Kristin's knuckles did a drum roll against the door. "Should I send in your meals? Tomorrow's paper? Next year's Christmas gifts?"

"Coming!" I laughed, turning off the shower. I dried off, then wrapped my hair in the towel. I'd

45

just put on my robe when someone pounded on the door again.

I threw it open. Steam swirled around me. "I said I was coming," I began, and stopped. Dillon. His eyes were still red, but this time, not from the pot.

"Thanks," he spit out, his voice low and furious. "Thanks a whole lot. What'd I ever do to you?" He whirled away.

I ran down the hall after him. "Dillon, wait." My turban slid off, and I clutched at it. "Dillon, I'm sorry! Really I am. I didn't mean to tell Dad. Honest. I was going to talk to you first, remember?"

"Oh, that helps a lot, *now.*" He turned to face me. "Thanks to you, I'm grounded for a week. A *week.* I can take my surfing lessons, but that's it. I'm stuck here. Just me and the coconuts. Whoopee."

I slumped against the wall. "Dillon, I'm so sorry. I wasn't going to tell Dad. It's just I was so mad about—oh, I don't know. I wanted to say something to hurt him, but instead I hurt you. I'm really sorry," I repeated.

"I guess I'm supposed to say it's okay, huh? Well, it isn't. It stinks. Leave me alone, will you?" Dillon stomped off to the sun porch, then hesitated in the middle of the room as if at a loss for something. If I hadn't felt so awful, I probably would've laughed. Dillon was the only one in our family who really showed his anger. When he was mad, you *knew* it from the noise. Poor kid! Now that Kristin and I had his bedroom, Dillon didn't even have a door to slam.

On the way back to the bathroom, I passed Dad

in the hall. He stopped me with a tentative hand on my shoulder.

"He'll be over it by tomorrow," he said. "He's more mad at himself than at you."

I nodded, knowing Dad was right. Dillon's anger was like striking a match. Burning fast and furious for that first millisecond, cooling almost immediately. With a sudden ache of gratitude, I reached out to touch Dad's hand. Then I pulled back, pretending to steady my towel.

The moment passed. Dad shoved his hands in his pockets. "I meant to tell you earlier, before you make plans for tomorrow, Patsy wants you up at the beach shack around nine."

"I work Sundays?"

Dad shook his head. "Monday through Friday, but you need to be shown the ropes. It'll only take a few minutes. Kristin can go along, too. Dillon's surfing lesson is at nine, so I'll drop off all three of you."

"Okay." I went back to the bedroom. My steps thudded a little more happily on the tiled floor. Working tomorrow, even for a short time, excited me. Lying on the beach was fun sometimes, but I really preferred *doing* things. Having an organized schedule. A plan of action. In that way, I was like Mom. She hadn't taken a vacation in years. "Why bother?" she'd said once, pointing to her head, "when there's so much excitement going on up here?" Even her trip to Europe had a purpose: She was going to a major art exhibition in Paris.

I put on a cool nightgown, then got into bed, relieved that the day was finally over. I'd let too many things get to me. But tomorrow would be different. I was determined to act friendlier to Jane,

47

try to make things right with Dillon, and have a great time with Kristin. And as for Dad, well, I'd be polite but cool. That was enough.

My plan of action was set. Now I could relax. I was reaching for Kristin's *Glamour* magazine, when she came back from her shower.

"Oh, no, you don't," she said, moving the magazine from my reach. "You'll just start analyzing the ads again."

I grinned sheepishly, then told her about going up to Kapakai the next morning.

"Great!" Kristin said. She snuggled between the sheets. "But afterward I want to go sight-seeing. Then I want to meet a few thousand gorgeous guys. And *then* I'm going to buy some postcards. Everybody I know in the world is going to get a postcard!"

That's what I liked about Kristin. She always had a plan of action, too.

The next morning Kristin and I both awoke at six, which was nine a.m. San Francisco time. Since I hadn't eaten dinner, I gobbled down two bowls of cereal. Then we went to the beach for a quick swim. It had rained the night before; the sand was damp and cool under our feet. The sky glowed a warm blue as the sun rose over the hills. Already I could feel its heat playing across my shoulders.

It was nearly nine when Kristin and I got back to the house. Dad and Dillon were waiting for us outside, the truck engine idling.

"We can't go yet," I said, panicking. "I have to put on a skirt and make-up."

Dad smiled. "This isn't San Francisco. Just wear

shorts and a T-shirt over that bathing suit and you'll
be fine.''

''But—''

''Hurry,'' Dillon insisted, his voice cross. ''I
don't wanna be late.''

''Okay.'' Kristin and I climbed into the back of
the truck.

Dillon stuck his head out of the passenger window and shouted, ''Hey, watch out for my surfboard.''

Obviously, he was still mad. But when we
reached Kapakai a few minutes later, his tone
brightened.

''There's the beach shack,'' he said. ''See? On
the other side of those condos. Come on, I want
you to meet Patsy.'' Surfboard under his arm, he
jogged across the grass toward a small white building that looked like a tool shed. There were about
a hundred beach chairs stacked next to it, and a
bin filled with white towels.

''Patsy!'' Dillon called. ''Hey, Pats.''

''Hi, Menehune.''

A tall guy in faded swim trunks came out of the
shack, carrying a head-high pile of towels. Hold
on, I thought. Patsy is a *guy?* Then he put down
the armload of towels and I got a look at his face.
Sunglasses!

I stared hard at myself in his reflecting frames.
''You're my boss?'' I blurted.

''You're Dillon's sister?'' He said it in almost
the same tone, but I could tell he was teasing.

My cheeks flushed. ''I—I thought you were a
girl.''

''Hmmm. I don't think so. Though someone did
whistle at my legs yesterday.''

49

Dillon laughed convulsively with the adoration of a younger brother. "Patsy's just a nickname," he explained, still chortling. "His real name's Patterson."

Sunglasses smiled. "A bit formal for Hawaii." He reached for my hand and shook it, holding it long enough for me to feel its warmth. Deep inside I felt a strange, exciting flutter. Oh, no, I thought. I *can't* like him. This guy had smoked pot with Dillon . . . was probably even the one who'd started him on the stuff.

He pulled away first and turned to Dad. "How ya doin', Marc?"

They shook hands warmly. "So, you already know these two young ladies, huh? Listen, how's that buddy of yours?" I stared at Dad. He sounded so different. So *friendly.* He and Sunglasses walked a few feet away, talking about some guy Dad had stitched up after a surfing accident.

Kristin and I sat down on the grass. "You're drooling again," I said.

Mesmerized by Sunglasses, Kristin automatically touched her lips with a finger. "I am not," she said, surprised, as if having really believed me. "Wow. 'The loser' is your *boss.* "

"I know." I flopped onto my stomach. "Did I have him pegged, or what? No wonder he's so tan. Spends his days here handing out towels. At night, he probably tends his pot forest. And in twenty years he'll be doing the same things. Only he won't understand why his brain's turned to rotten seaweed."

"Your dad and Dillon seem to love him."

"Yeah, well." I plucked at a clump of grass.

"I'm gonna see that Dillon drops this loser real quick."

A shadow fell across my back. "Dillon makes his own choices," Sunglasses said.

I sat up, my face growing hot. We stared at each other for a minute, as if in a showdown. Then Sunglasses said, his voice low and casual, "Ready for your orientation?"

6

I left Kristin sitting on the grass and followed Sunglasses into the beach shack. My face felt on fire. I was embarrassed he'd overheard my comments, and angry at my embarrassment. What bugged me even more was his reaction. With the exception of what I'd said about Dillon, Sunglasses acted as if my words didn't matter. As if *I* didn't matter. I'd never seen a pothead with that kind of self-control. Or that kind of loyalty to anyone, especially somebody else's brother.

"Well, this is the office," Sunglasses was saying. "Snorkeling equipment is stored here, surfboards out back. I post the work schedules on that cork board. Check them weekly. First-aid kit here, radio, telephone, and minirefrigerator. Please bring your own sodas. Any questions so far?"

I shook my head, not trusting my voice.

"If you haven't noticed yet," Sunglasses continued, "this is a cake job. When guests want to check out something, like chairs, towels, beach stuff, just make sure they put their name and room number on that sheet." He pointed to a clipboard hanging on the back of the shack door. "When they return stuff, cross of their names. Piece of cake, right? Hard part's being nice to everybody, all day and every day. This job is mainly public relations for the resort. So you've got to turn on the charm. And give each man, woman, and child—even the nasty, complaining ones—a friendly, aloha smile." He flashed a sincere grin, his teeth looking very white against his tanned face. Then he stroked his chin for a second, studying me. "Uh, you *do* know how to smile, don't you?"

"Sure."

"Mind giving me a demonstration?"

"You mean, you want me to smile right now?"

"Yeah. Right now. Right here." He poked his head out the door. "Nobody's watching. What's the holdup? You need Bill Cosby to get you going?"

I couldn't help it. I laughed.

"That'll do," Sunglasses said. He strolled back outside. "You also need to be on time. That's the one flaw with a cake job. People get bored. Lazy. Sometimes we overlap shifts so that you have another worker to talk to, and that helps. Here comes one of your co-workers now."

A girl wearing a pastel pink bikini with ruffles sprinted toward us across the lawn. Her long brown hair streamed behind her, tangling in the handles of a straw bag that jostled over one shoulder.

"Hel-lo, gorgeous," she sang breathlessly. "Sorry I'm late. I closed the club last night with some of your buddies. Didn't get home till almost three and slept clean through my alarm. You're not going to fire me, are you?" She looked up at him from under a fringe of lashes, almost, but not quite, fluttering them. Before he could answer, she said,

53

"Thanks, you're a sweetie. Now where did I put my T-shirt?" She dug through her bag, scattering fashion magazines, suntan lotion, a hair brush, and two cans of diet Coke. With a yelp, she finally pulled out a cotton aqua tee that read KAPAKAI across the front. She jerked it on, scooped everything back into her bag, grinned, and said: "Okay, I'm ready!"

Sunglasses laughed. "Drew, this is Kelli. She works weekends and fills in now and then during the week. Kell, Drew's taking over Chip's morning spot."

"Hi." Kelli gave me a quick, polite smile, as if she was meeting someone's grandmother, then flashed it back full-force on Patsy. Obviously, a terminal crush. I wondered if the feeling was mutual. Then I wondered why I cared.

I turned to find Kristin lying under a palm tree a few feet away. She put a hand on one hip and fluttered her eyelashes in a perfect imitation of Kelli.

I stifled a laugh and mouthed, *You are so bad!* Kristin only winked.

"Kell, take over," Sunglasses said. "Surf lesson time. Drew, would you come help me pick out a board?" We walked to the back of the shack. "Here, this one looks about your size."

"Wait a sec." I grabbed his arm. "Why do *I* need a surfboard?"

"Little hard to surf without one."

"What?!"

Sunglasses laughed. "All part of the job, Drew. If I get sick, you have to give the lessons. No big deal. Just show little kids the basics, like how to stand up, how to fall off." He handed me a sleek

54

fiberglass board. "Don't panic. It's not as if we're surfing fifteen-footers at Sunset Beach. The waves inside the reef are two feet at best. But it gives the kids a real thrill. Come on."

I didn't move. "Look, I don't think I can handle this."

Sunglasses kept walking. "You mean you don't *want* to handle it."

"That's not it. I'm not a very good swimmer and—"

"Drew." Sunglasses turned to face me. The sun reflected off his silver shades, blinding me for a second. "Drew, you either learn how to surf or lose the job. I don't like being a hard case about this, but there are a dozen other people waiting for this job if you can't hack it."

For a brief moment, I considered bailing. Anything would be better than working for Sunglasses. Except, once Kristin left, I'd have nothing to do the rest of the summer. And boredom took a close second to heights in my book of hates.

"Okay," I agreed. "Fine. I'll give it a try. But only if you teach Kristin to surf, too."

Sunglasses shrugged. "Okay by me. Hey, Kristin!" He motioned for her to come over. "Grab a surfboard."

"Sure!"

The three of us headed for the water's edge. Dillon was waiting for us, doing leg-stretches in the sand. Two tow-headed kids, who looked about six or seven, sat next to him, trying hard to imitate his movements. I didn't see Dad anywhere and figured he must have gone back to the house.

"All set, guys?" Sunglasses asked. The kids nodded ecstatically. "Okay, tell me your names and then we'll get started. Allen and Ashleigh? Hi, I'm Patsy. Before we get in the water, we're gonna practice how to stand on our boards.'' Sunglasses pulled his T-shirt off over his head and tossed it beside Dillon. Hands on his hips, he glanced at my brother. ''Hey, Menehune, what are you doing here? You don't need lessons anymore.''

Dillon cocked his head in surprise. ''But, Patsy—''

''No 'buts.' You don't need me. Now get out of here. I want to see you out there with the pros, surfing First Break.'' He pointed to the large waves that rose high and rough against a far reef.

With a grin, Dillon picked up the velcro leash dangling from his board and attached it to an ankle. Then he charged into the water, slid onto his board and paddled smoothly, expertly ducking under the larger waves.

I felt a shiver of fear. ''Are you sure he's ready for that?'' I asked Sunglasses.

''He's ready.'' He clapped his hands once. ''Okay, let's get goin' here.''

For the next ten minutes, he showed us the simple basics of surfing: How to stand sideways, how to bend our knees, how to balance with our arms. Allen and Ashleigh listened patiently, their brows furled in concentration. Kristin looked fascinated. I had to admit, it was pretty interesting. At least, until Sunglasses, a wry smile pulling at his lips, had us lie down on our boards to practice paddling in the sand.

Suddenly, I felt silly. A group of sunbathers were watching us. When they began to snicker I said, ''Can't we try this in the water now?''

''Sure,'' Sunglasses said, his smile widening.

"We'll practice on that little reef, away from the swimmers and the larger waves. I won't be surfing, but I'll swim out with you and give you a push when a swell comes."

Kristin and I watched as Sunglasses helped Allen and Ashleigh ease their boards into the water. Then the four of us paddled out, Sunglasses swimming behind.

"Who wants to go first?" he asked when we reached the reef.

Before anyone had a chance to speak he continued, "Drew? Good. Okay, here comes a wave. I'll give you a push when it's time. But *don't* stand up. Just coast along on your stomach. Get a feel for the speed you'll be traveling. Here you go!"

Sunglasses pushed. I felt the wave catch me. Then I was sailing along, clutching the sides of the board, cool water threading up over its nose to embroider across my face. This wasn't so hard. Sunglasses had been babying us all morning. Probably just to humiliate Kris and me. I bet I could stand without any problem.

I pushed up with my arms to my knees. My feet. Then I straightened—and freaked. I was traveling so fast! Streaking straight for the beach. And I'd forgotten how to stop. I was going to crash. Or fall off—

So I jumped.

The water rose to meet me. My left foot throbbed as it scraped against the sharp lava reef. I cried out and swallowed a mouthful of salt water. Coughing and sputtering, I struggled to the shore where my board had beached itself. Three little boys were trying to drag it away. I glared at them and they scattered, giggling. Hurt and humiliated,

I heaved the board into the water, and paddled back out to my group.

"Well done, Drew," Sunglasses said. "Kids, Drew just graciously demonstrated for you the *wrong* way to fall. Now remember, try to fall *flat*—" he did a horizontal flop with the flat of his hand, *"not* straight up and down. Okay, Allen, here you go."

"You're bleeding!" Kristin said, her eyes wide.

"It's nothing," I mumbled, trying to avoid Sunglasses' gaze. But my foot felt like thick sliced bacon. It pulsated with pain.

"Keep it under the water," Sunglasses advised. "Salt's good for it."

"I won't attract sharks, will I? I can just imagine hundreds of fish closing in for a taste of foot sushi."

Sunglasses laughed. "No. Don't worry. I'll take care of it when we're finished here. Hey, don't look so embarrassed. You can't expect to be Margo Oberg your first time out."

"Who's Margo Oberg?" Kristin asked.

Ashleigh piped up, "Seven-Time Women's World Surfing Champion!"

"Atta girl, Ashleigh," Sunglasses said. "Okay, get ready, here's your wave! Kristin, you're next."

We continued to practice. Allen and Ashleigh caught on right away, probably because they weren't old enough to know they were supposed to be scared. After a half hour, Sunglasses allowed them to surf alone, a few yards away from us. Then he concentrated on Kristin and me. Soon even Kristin was standing—wobbling, but standing—and riding swells all the way to the shore. I was the only bozo in the bunch. Despite Sunglasses' directions and shouts of encouragement, every time I stood up, I'd freak out about the height and the speed and jump off.

"Look, this is pointless," I said at last. I was breathing hard, and my arms ached. "We've been at this an hour. I'm just wasting my time. And yours."

Sunglasses was standing chest-high in the water. His arm rested on my board, holding it steady. "You're catchin' on to the basics, Drew," he said, "and that's never a waste." He turned toward me. Our faces were very close. Almost touching.

Feeling self-conscious, I glanced down. My gaze traveled along his arm, noticing its blond hairs against the tanned wet skin, then moved up to his waterproof watch. It was black and velcroed snug around his wrist. He had broad hands, the fingers long and sculptured. Nails slightly bitten, but neat. Nice. Nice hands.

Something fluttered deep inside me. I wanted to reach out, feel that hand holding mine again. Then, just as fast, I remembered yesterday. That same hand had taken the joint from Dillon's fingers.

"No," I said aloud. The force in my voice surprised me. "I'm ready to quit."

Sunglasses stood so still that I could hear the water lapping against my board. "Okay," he began, "but Drew, we're going to be working together all summer, so I'd like to find out one thing. Why do you dislike me so much?"

I'm sure my mouth dropped open. "Are you always so honest?" I asked.

"Are you always so evasive?"

"Well, no. I mean—"

"Look, if something's bothering you, just tell

me. There's nothing I hate more than guessing games, unless it's the silent treatment. So let's be up-front with each other, okay?''

''Okay.'' I took a deep breath. Then the words rushed out in a spasm of anger. ''I don't like how you're influencing my brother. I saw you yesterday, at Brennecke's. Watched you put your arm around him, real buddy-buddy like, and share his joint. Maybe you didn't start him on the stuff, but he really looks up to you. Smoking with him will only make him think it's okay. And—and I think that's a pretty rotten thing to do to a thirteen-year-old kid.'' I started to paddle away. ''I'm going in now. Thanks for the lesson.''

''Whoa, there, Jezebel.'' Sunglasses grabbed my foot and pulled me back. ''You're like a hit-and-run driver, you know that? Give me a chance to set you straight on what really happened yesterday, okay?''

I glared at him, but waited.

''Okay, you did see me put my arm around Dillon,'' Sunglasses continued. ''But it wasn't a friendly hey-let-me-have-a-toke gesture. More of a what-the-hell-you-doin'? grip, like this.'' His arm slid across my shoulders, firm fingers taking hold of the back of my neck for a second, like somebody picking up a naughty puppy. ''I took that joint from Dillon to throw it *away,* Drew. Did you actually see me smoke it?''

I thought back, then shook my head.

Sunglasses continued, ''I care enough about Dillon to see that he stays off it. He's a special kid, Drew.''

''I know.'' My throat ached. I was afraid I might cry. I turned my head, searching for Dillon on the horizon. There he was. Shearing down the face of a wave. Then, with precisioned grace, he cut back and up, away from the wave as it exploded in foam against the reef. Perfect.

I shook my head in amazement. His body had looked so taut, so in control. Had I been wrong about Dillon? Wrong about the control in his life, his choice of friends, his decision to stay with Dad? Wrong about Sunglasses?

"I wouldn't ever do anything to hurt your brother," Sunglasses said. He pushed his silver frames up onto his head and for the first time, I saw his eyes. They didn't have that red-glazed look of a pothead. A little sun-strained maybe, but otherwise clear and gray.

"I believe you," I said. "I—I'm really sorry, Sunglasses."

His eyes narrowed, amused, at the nickname. Then he laughed and the lenses covered his eyes again. "Thanks. Just for that apology, I'll let you quit now." A pause. "After one more wave."

"Oh, no!" I couldn't control it. I started laughing too, in great gulps of relief. It had felt so good to get all that anger out. And I hadn't once felt that falling sensation, like I did with Dad. What was the difference? Was it because Sunglasses was a stranger? Or because he had forced me to confront him, something Dad would never do?

I didn't have time to figure it out. The next thing I knew, Sunglasses had shouted "Go!" and given me a great push. The wave swept me along. And then I was standing, cool and calm. Riding the board toward shore as if I'd been doing it for years. Surfing!

"That was perfect," Sunglasses said later, when he put our boards away. "Well done, Drew."

My chest filled with pride. "Thanks. I couldn't have done it without your expert teaching."

"Aw, shucks, ma'am. 'Twas nuthin'." He gave my arm a quick squeeze. "Enough of this Mutual Admiration Society. Go rinse off that foot. The faucet is over there. I'll get the first-aid kit."

Kristin pulled me aside. "Hey, Drew," she said with a sly smile and a nudge, "I think Patsy *likes* you!"

"Kristin, get real. We're friends, that's all."

"Don't give me that 'just friends' stuff. You like him too. Admit it!"

"I think he'll make a very nice boss," I said.

"I think he'd make a very nice boyfriend," she shot back.

"Yeah, maybe for Kelli. She's got her eye on him, remember?"

"True. But the big question is," Kristin answered, wiggling her eyebrows, "does he have his eye on *her*. Stay tuned!"

I waved her away and bent to look at my foot. I'd never had a boyfriend. And I didn't want one now. I liked the idea of knowing guys as casual friends. Buddies. People to pal around with now and then. That seemed easier, less scary, somehow. And yet . . .

Yet when I thought of Sunglasses, an inexplicable wave of excitement rippled through me, like the day before when I'd first stepped off the plane.

7

"Why are you walking so slow?" Dillon complained as the three of us headed back to the beach house.

Kristin groaned. "Come on, Dill, give us a break! We just surfed for the first time. My legs feel like rubber bands. No, more like soggy spaghetti. And Margo Oberg here cut her foot."

"You *did?*" Dillon forgot to act mad at me for a minute. His voice held a hint of admiration. "You really cut yourself surfing?"

"Ouch. Yes." Every other step I took felt as if I had a shoe full of cactus. Soon I developed a rhythm. *Step, Ouch, Limp. Step, Ouch, Limp.*

"Did Patsy bandage it for you?"

"Yep." And how! While Kelli had stood by glaring, his strong hands swabbed the stinging cut with soft cotton and antiseptic. Then, gently holding my ankle, he smoothed on the bandage.

"Wear that wound with pride, Drew," he said, giving my foot a final pat. "You're a true surfer once you've christened a foot or a knee or your head." He fingered a small knot on the bridge of his nose. "See you tomorrow. Nine o'clock sharp."

I'd be there all right, even if I had to crawl!

Step, Ouch, Limp. By the time we reached home it was almost noon.

"There you are," Jane called. Kneeling in a flower bed, trowel in hand, she squinted up at us with a smile. Her cheeks were pink with exertion. "Just dealing with a few stubborn weeds. Marc's over there, pruning his bonzai trees. Ready for lunch? I made chicken salad." She stood, peeling off her gardening gloves. "Afterward, Marc and I thought we'd take you sight-seeing. Maybe go up to Napali Lookout and Waimea Canyon, or—Drew! You're limping! What happened?"

I remembered Sunglasses' words. "Oh, nothing," I said with exaggerated modesty. "Just cut myself surfing."

"Maybe I should take a look at it." Dad strolled over, wearing his 'concerned doctor' expression.

"No, thanks," I said. "It's all taken care of."

"If you cut it on coral, infection could set in. . . ."

"It's *fine*, Dad."

Silence. He visibly backed down.

"Well—" Jane interrupted. She brushed at the dirt on her shorts, but only succeeded in smudging it. "We'd better eat and get going. It's an hour's drive to the canyon."

"What is Waimea Canyon?" Kristin asked.

"The Grand Canyon of the Pacific," Jane said, as if quoting a guide book. "It's a gorge. Not as big as the Grand Canyon, but the colors! Greens, hot blues, burnt orange. They're breathtaking."

"Can I come?" Dillon asked.

"You may not." Dad's voice was stern. "You're grounded, remember? There are plenty of chores around here for you to finish. Besides," his tone softened, "you've seen the canyon dozens of times."

"Yeah, yeah, yeah." Dillon stormed into the house.

Limping as fast as I could, I followed him to the sun porch. He was lying on the daybed, hands behind his head, staring at the ceiling.

"Dillon?"

"Go away."

I perched on the edge of the bed. "Hey, I'm sorry you can't go sight-seeing with us. You really wanted to be the one to show me the canyon, didn't you?" No response. "Well, maybe after Kristin leaves, you and I could go see it again, just the two of us. Or maybe—"

"I said, go away."

I grew impatient. "Listen, Dillon. I'm sorry you're grounded. But I'm *not* sorry Dad found out about the pot. Maybe I shouldn't have told him, but Dillon, you're my brother. I care about you. And I just don't want to see you get messed up."

Dillon turned his face to the wall. What had happened to the little brother I used to hug and hold and protect? The brother who wanted to be hugged and held and only by me?

I limped away.

Dillon taunted: "Hey Druid, you forgot to leave your shoes outside."

I peeked back around the door frame. "Yeah? Well, so did *you!*"

A surprised silence. Then a thong came sailing across the room. Just missed my nose. I leaped

65

back, laughing, and thought I heard a snicker. Dillon and I would be all right.

After lunch, Kristin and I washed the dishes. We had just sponged the last crumbs into the garbage disposal when Jane came into the kitchen. "Ready to go?" she asked, jangling her keys. She had a sweatshirt draped over one arm and was wearing a sunvisor. "Better bring along sweaters," she added. "Sometimes it gets chilly up at the Lookout."

We called good-bye to Dillon. He grunted in reply. Dad was already outside, sitting in the passenger seat of the Subaru. Kris and I climbed in the back.

Within a few minutes we had reached the old, one-block-long town of Koloa. Then Jane turned left, heading to the west side of the island.

"Everything's so beautiful," Kristin said. Perched on the edge of the seat, her head stuck out the open window, she reminded me of an overgrown puppy ready for her first ride.

"Here," Jane said, handing a map over her shoulder. "This'll give you an idea of where we're headed."

Kris unfolded the map over our knees. "Oh, Drew, don't you just love the names of these towns? See, we just passed Ka-la-heeo . . ."

"Hey-o," Jane corrected.

"Right. Next is Ha-na-pee-pee."

"Pay-pay."

"Yeah, and then we come to Kau—uh, wait a sec, Jane, don't help me—Kau-mak . . . oh, forget it."

I chimed in. "Cow-ma-ka-knee?"

"Easy for you to say," Kristin grumbled.

Jane smiled into the rearview mirror. "Not bad, guys. Try pronouncing each vowel as a separate syllable, with the accent on the next-to-last syllable, like this. . . ."

As we wound up the twisty road to the canyon, Jane taught us a few words. I caught on quickly, but the only word Kristin mastered was *kapu,* which means Keep Out, or Forbidden. Every time Jane coaxed her to say a new and longer word, Kristin would shout *kapu! kapu!* until I was laughing so hard my stomach ached. Dad even turned around once and favored us with his slow smile.

"Oh-oh," Jane said a few minutes later. "We're running into a little mist. Change of plans. We'll hit the canyon on our way back down and see Napali Lookout first. It's higher up. If we don't get there before the clouds do, we won't see a thing."

Jane down-shifted. The Subaru whined as we climbed higher. I slipped a cotton sweater over my head. The air coming in the open windows felt almost chilly now.

"Here we are." Jane buzzed into a large parking lot. Before she could tug on the emergency brake, Kristin and I were out the door, she racing, me limping, up the hill to the Lookout. A few people with cameras stood at the metal railing. They turned to glance at us, faces unable to hide their disappointment.

"Nothing to see," grumbled one man. "Too cloudy." He and his group moved to go.

"Oh, rats!" Kristin banged the handrail.

"Give it time," Dad said, coming up behind us. He and Jane were arm in arm. "The mist might clear. I already see a patch of blue over there."

"We've waited a half hour," the man complained.

Dad shrugged. "We'll take the chance."

Kristin and I peered over the railing into a sea of fog. The cold damp air seemed to seep into my bones. I pulled my sweater closer. "What's down there, anyway?" I asked.

"Kalalau Valley," Jane said. "Part of the Napali Coast. It's four thousand feet straight down. Some people call it the Lost Valley because there's no road to it. The only way in is by helicopter, boat, or a two-day, eleven-mile backpack."

She snuggled under Dad's arm. "In May, Marc and I camped back there for two weeks. It's a treacherous trail, but worth it. We camped by a waterfall and had a beach all to ourselves. It was very romantic. . . ." Her voice trailed off. Dad had bent to kiss her, his hand cupping her cheek. Jane's sunvisor threw a shadow across their faces, but I caught a glimpse of Dad's smile. He looked so happy.

I jerked my gaze away. I felt somehow trapped, like when my bedcovers were tucked too tightly around me. I moved closer to Kristin. My hands gripped the rail.

I suddenly, vividly remembered another time when Dad had kissed someone that way. Three years ago, during out last vacation as a family . . .

"Marc, I just got a call from the gallery," Mom says, coming toward us across the beach.

We're at Cape Cod. Dad and Dillon are building a sandcastle. I'm wet from swimming, and covering myself with hot sand. When I'm all coated, I'll chase Dillon into the water, pretending I'm the abominable sandmonster.

"Sounds serious," says Dad.

"It is." A sigh. "It's the Schloss exhibition. I'm going to have to fly back right away."

Dad is quiet for a long time. "This is our first real vacation in almost five years," he says at last. "We've both been working so hard. We need the rest."

"I know. But the gallery's in an uproar. This exhibition is very important."

"Can't you wait just a few more days? The drive back to San Francisco will only take a week. Five days, max, if we drive nonstop."

Mom shakes her head. "I've got to get back, Marc."

I can't believe Mom won't be driving home with us. At times the cross-country trip was gross, especially when Dillon barfed. But mostly we had fun. Mom and Dad sang silly words to radio commercials. Lots of times Dad pretended to be lost and would toss me maps of Australia and Fresno and France, saying, "Drew, can you find Texas for me, please?" And once, Dad turned on the cruise control and drove with both his feet hanging out the window. Dillon and I laughed so loud Mom woke up wide-eyed, and choked, "Marc, what are you doing?!"

"You'd better take the kids," Dad is saying. "If they stay with me, it'll be rough driving cross-country without your help. Especially if Dillon has an asthma attack."

"All right. You know how sorry I am about this, don't you, honey? We'll try to get away next month. Just the two of us." Mom looks over at

69

me. "Hey, Mrs. Sandman. How'd you like to fly home tomorrow?"

"Great!" I leap up, scattering sand everywhere like a big clumsy dog. Flying is even better than driving. Listening to the movies and rock music with those little earphones. Staring out the window at snow-covered mountains and acres of farmland that look like green patchwork quilts. And those electric blue lights that glow eerily along the runway at night. We're flying home! I can hardly wait.

But the next morning at the airport, something finally sinks in. Dad isn't coming with us.

He gives Dillon and me a big hug and a smile at the gate. And then he bends to kiss Mom. He cups her cheek with a hand and looks down into her eyes. I expect to see love there, like in all those romantic movies. But a shadow crosses his face. He looks like a stranger. A sad, lonely stranger.

Mom tugs on my arm. I follow her and Dillon up the ramp, into the plane and to our seats. When the plane takes off, I start to cry. I try to hide the hot tears, but Mom hears me sniffling and pulls me close. "What's wrong?" she murmurs. "What's wrong, Drew?" But I can't talk. Can't tell her I'm afraid. I'm fourteen years old, yet I'm afraid of a stupid, silly shadow I've seen briefly on Dad's face.

"Drew," Kristin whispered.

I shook my head to clear the memory of Dad and shadows from my mind. Kris was pointing down. "Drew, look!"

The mist of Kalalau Valley had begun to swirl around us. It drifted up in eerie silence. I saw sharp, moss green fingers jabbing through the clouds . . . a glimpse of liquid blue sky—or was it the sea?—and a flash of sunshine. Then, with one great breath, a brisk wind scattered the mist and clouds. The view was clear in a sudden flood of sun and color. The earth fell away one step, two, from where I stood. Only a metal rail kept me from plunging down the fluted cliffs, off the edge to the lost world below.

My stomach leaped. Cold sweat broke across my forehead. I gripped the handrail tighter, my breath coming in shallow gasps. *Oh, God*, I thought. *Don't let me fall. . . .*

I heard a buzzing in my ears. Dad's face loomed before me, his mouth working, but I couldn't hear. The buzzing grew to a roar. Dad's face faded in a dizzy sparkle of tiny suns. Everything went white, then black. I was going down.

"Drew? Drew!"

I found myself sitting on the ground, head between my legs. The grass looked blurred, but the roaring sound had faded. I blinked. When the grass sharpened into focus, I started to lift my head, but a hand pushed gently against my hair. "No, stay down for a second, Drew," Dad murmured. "If you move too fast, you might faint again."

"I'm okay." My voice sounded hoarse but firm.

"What happened?" Kristin asked.

"I think she hyperventilated," Dad said. "She was staring over the cliff and then suddenly—"

"I'm okay now. I just need some water." I struggled to stand.

"Let me help." Dad put out an arm.

"No, I'm all right. Please don't fuss." With shaky steps, I headed back to the parking lot.

"Don't be silly, Drew." Jane hurried beside me, put an arm around my shoulders. "I'll help you to the car, then get you a drink. There's a thermos stowed under the seat and I think I saw a fountain near the restrooms."

My legs felt like Jell-O. Gratefully, I leaned against Jane's small body. She was surprisingly strong and supported me down the hill. I half-collapsed in the backseat of the car. By the time Jane brought me the cup of tepid water, I felt much better.

"I feel so stupid," I mumbled.

"There's nothing to feel stupid about," Jane said in a matter-of-fact tone. She hunched down in the gravel lot, one hand toying with a few pebbles at her feet. "It's a frightening cliff. A height like that can make all of us a little panicky." She looked up at me, her voice soft. "Or has this happened to you before?"

I swallowed. "How did you know?"

"Because when you came out of that faint, you weren't surprised in the least. Just defensive. And angry." She let a handful of pebbles sift through her fingers. "What kind of high places usually bother you?"

I shrugged. Took another sip of water. "All of them," I said finally. "Cliffs, tall buildings, bridges. And airplanes. Especially airplanes."

"Did you ever have a bad experience on a plane?"

"You mean like crashing or something?"

"No, nothing that drastic. Just something that made you feel out of control. Trapped. Closed in."

That's exactly how I feel, I thought in wonder. Not only in high places, but in certain situations, too. Like watching Dad and Jane kiss. I hated that, yet there wasn't a thing I could do about it.

72

I stiffened. "You're not trying to analyze me, are you?" Then, hearing anger in my voice, I tried to disguise it with a joke. "Because if you are, well, I probably can't afford you."

Jane chuckled. "No," she said, shaking her head. "I'm only trying to get you to think about *why* you're afraid of heights, not just that you are. Sometimes knowing what causes our fears makes them a little easier to handle."

"Oh." I leaned against the seat, my eyes closed. I couldn't shake the sensation of falling, of looking down over the dizzying edge of that cliff.

Jane patted my arm. "We'll go soon. Kristin said something about wanting pictures. Try to relax. Would you like to talk some more?"

Without opening my eyes, I shook my head. After a moment, I heard the sound of crunching gravel as Jane walked away. I didn't want to talk. I didn't want to think. I just wanted to get back down the mountain. Back to solid, flat earth. Back where I felt safe.

8

"Can I go with you to Kapakai?" Kristin asked me over breakfast the next morning. The warm sun shone through the slats of the kitchen's wood mini-blinds, striping her face like a zebra. On the counter, the coffeemaker chuckled.

"I can read and sunbathe while you work," Kris continued. "Maybe Patsy will even let me help check out towels and stuff."

"Sure," I said. "That'd be great! I thought of asking you, but was afraid you'd get bored." I munched on my last piece of toast. I felt good today. In less than an hour I'd be starting a new job. Seeing Sunglasses again. And yesterday's episode at Napali had been shoved into a mental closet, the door slammed and locked.

"I'm *never* bored," Kristin announced. She took a bite of bacon, then licked her fingers. "At least, I won't be if we can buy postcards on the way."

"Deal. Let's go." I drained the last of my guava juice and started to clear the table.

"No, no, leave those," Jane said, scurrying barefoot into the kitchen. She wore a pale yellow sundress with a white linen blazer. "Old Hawaiian

74

custom: on work days we wash all the dishes once and once only, *after* dinner." She took two mugs from the cupboard and poured coffee in each. The rich aroma filled the room.

"Is that really a Hawaiian custom?" Kristin asked.

"No. Mine. I've been late to work too many times trying to win the 'Miss Housework' award. So now I just don't bother to bother." Jane picked up both mugs. "See you tonight, girls. Oh, by the way. You can borrow our bikes, if you'd like. They're in the shed out back. Might be easier than walking on that foot, Drew. Now what did I do with my shoes? Marc! We're going to be late!" She hurried out of the kitchen, coffee dribbling on the floor.

"I like her," Kristin said. "Don't you?"

"She's okay."

"Oh, come on, Drew. How can you not like her?"

I smiled and swiped at the coffee dribbles with a paper towel. "Kind of a slob."

"Well, not everyone's as perfect as your mother."

"I thought you liked my mother," I said.

"Well, I don't." Kristin folded her arms and looked me square in the eye. Then she grinned. "I *love* her. She's wonderful. Beautiful, talented, a class act. And a hard one for Jane to follow."

"The harder the better," I murmured.

"You're not being very fair."

I tossed the paper towel into the wastebasket. "Who's been fair to my mom?"

"I know, I know." Kristin sighed. "But I'll bet

75

Jane hurts, too. You know, when Dillon or your dad mention your mom's name.''

"Maybe, but I doubt it. Jane's a counselor, Kris. She's trained to handle that kind of stuff.''

"But, Drew, she still has *feelings*. When she hurts, she can't just take two therapies and call herself in the morning!''

I laughed in agreement. "I know, I know. Come on.''

Kristin followed me down the hall to our bedroom. I picked up my backpack, double-checking to see if my wallet and keys were inside, then slung it across my shoulders. "If we're gonna stop and get postcards,'' I said, "we'd better hurry. First day on the job. Good impressions with the boss and all that.''

Kristin slipped her towel into my pack. "I think you already made a good impression with the 'boss.' I wonder if he'll ask you out?''

My heart skipped a beat. "I doubt it. Don't you remember Kelli? The way she glared at me? If looks could kill, I'd have been cremated. No, I'm pretty sure Sunglasses belongs to her.''

"Hmm. Or at least she *thinks* so,'' Kristin said. "Like I said before, we'll just have to make sure. Onward, ho!''

As Jane had promised, we found two ten-speeds in the shed behind the house. Both were old and clunky, but the gears shifted fine. It only took us a few minutes to pedal to Poipu Beach Hotel, just a couple of blocks away from Kapakai. Their gift shop had just opened.

I bought two postcards of Poipu Beach, one for Mom and one to send to my friends at the ad agency. Kristin bought eighteen cards, six of which were pictures of Waimea Canyon. She stuffed them into my pack.

"It was so beautiful," she said, looking almost guilty. "I wish you'd seen it, too."

I had waited in the car the day before, when Dad, Kristin, and Jane stopped to admire the canyon. After having the anxiety attack at Napali Lookout, I decided I'd had enough of cliffs and canyons for one day.

"Don't apologize," I said to Kristin. "It's okay. I'll see the canyon another time." But I knew that wasn't true. I wouldn't go back to Waimea. Ever. The fear of having another attack was even stronger now than my fear of heights.

"Hey, you're early," Sunglasses said when we arrived at Kapakai a few minutes later. "I'm impressed. Keep it up every day and I'll get spoiled. Even worse, you'll deserve a raise."

He grinned at me. My insides turned to warm coconut pudding. "Uh—Kristin's going to hang out here with me, if that's okay. She wants to help. You won't have to pay her," I added.

"Slave labor—my favorite. Here, you can both start with these." He pointed to a pile of freshly laundered towels. "Fold and place them in that bin. People will be hitting the beach any second. Hey, Drew, how's that foot?"

Before I could answer, I spotted Dillon trotting across the lawn, surfboard under his arm. "Dillon! What are you doing here?"

He laid his board down in the grass. "Surfing lesson, remember?" Taking a piece of wax from the pocket of his swim trunks, he knelt down and began to wax the board, his arm moving in deft, circular strokes.

77

"But I thought you didn't need lessons anymore," I said. "Doesn't Dad know that?"

Dillon grimaced. "No. You won't tell him, will you, Druid? I've got to practice every day, or I'll get out of shape. I'll only stay an hour, as long as my lessons usually lasted. Then I'll go right back home. Please, don't rat on me, Drew. Dad'll ground me for the whole summer, if he finds out."

Sunglasses held up a hand. "Hold on, Menehune. What's going on? You got grounded? What for?"

Dillon didn't answer. Sunglasses glanced at me, then nodded. "Oh, the pot business, huh? Well, you earned that one. I guess you'd better head home."

"But Dad'll never know, Patsy," Dillon began.

"Yeah? And how 'bout when he pays me for the lessons? Do you expect me to take that money without working for it? Uh-uh. Your Dad's been straight and fair with me, and I want to do the same for him. But tell you what—" Sunglasses adjusted his frames with a push of a finger. "Talk to your Dad, Dillon. If he'll let you practice one hour a day up here, with me as a sort of chaperon, then that's okay. If not, well, I don't want to see you here till your sentence is up."

"Oh, all right." Dillon stood, hefting his surfboard. "If I go home, will you take me surfing at Shipwrecks next week?"

"No." Sunglasses studied his clipboard, jotting notes on it with a pencil stub. "I don't make deals like that, Dillon."

Dillon's face fell.

"But," Sunglasses continued, not looking up,

78

"I *will* take you to Shipwrecks because you're a nice kid."

Dillon beamed. "Oh-kay!" He hurried away, his leash trailing behind him in the grass.

"You really do like him, don't you?" I asked.

Sunglasses replaced the clipboard on its hook and started to help Kristin and me to fold towels. "Sure, I like him. I got pretty close to Dillon and your dad when I lived with them last fall. It was a rough time for me, but they helped a lot. Especially your dad. We had some good talks."

My hands froze in midfold. "Talks? You and Dad actually *talked?* What'd you do, slip truth serum into his coffee?" Then my mind absorbed something else. "Wait a sec. You *lived* with Dad and Dillon?"

"Mornin'," a voice boomed. We turned to see a heavyset man with a lobster red sunburn. Two kids hid behind his thick legs. "Is this where we get the chairs and towels?" he asked.

"Yes sir," Sunglasses said cheerfully. "These ladies will help you. . . ."

"How many towels do you need, sir?" Kristin asked with her pert smile. She led him over to the sign-up sheet.

Sunglasses touched my arm. "My morning's booked with surf lessons," he said. "But we'll talk later, okay?"

He sauntered toward the water. I watched the muscles play across his tanned back as he shifted a surfboard under each arm. Why had he lived with Dad and Dillon? I wondered. Didn't he have a family of his own? And how on earth had he gotten Dad to talk? The idea of him and Dad having a special conversation made me feel empty inside.

The morning went fast. Kristin and I handed out towels, sold suntan lotion, noted sign-ups for surf lessons and smiled, smiled, smiled. By noon I wasn't sure which hurt worse: my cheek muscles or the sunburn across my shoulders.

"Here comes Kelli," Kristin murmured at quarter past noon. "Now for the moment of truth."

Just then, Sunglasses wandered up. The hair on his legs was slicked down with salt water. Rivulets dripped from his glasses, off the end of his nose. He shook his head, sending cool droplets flying, then toweled himself off.

"Hi, Drew. Hi, Kristin," Kelli said. Then, in a breathless trill: "Hel-lo, Patsy."

"Hi, cutie," he replied.

Cutie!

Kelli practically glowed.

"Uh, Pats, could we talk to you a second?" Kristin asked. She slipped an arm through his, as if ready to lead him on a casual stroll. "Patsy, Drew and I were wondering if you'd like to come to dinner tonight. It's our turn to cook and Drew makes a mean coq au vin." She glanced over her shoulder at Kelli and added, her voice edged with friendly innocence, "That's French for chicken in wine, you know."

Kelli's smile wavered.

"Sounds delicious," Sunglasses said, "but I've already got a date tonight. How 'bout tomorrow? Could you switch dinners with whoever's cooking?"

"Sure. We can switch with Dillon, right, Drew?" Kristin nudged me. *"Right,* Drew?"

"Uh—right. Sure." I watched as Kelli's mouth shaped into a round O of surprise. I think I was just as shocked.

"Seven o'clock okay with you?" Kris asked.

Sunglasses nodded. "I'll be there. See you tomorrow. For work *and* dinner."

We got our bikes and had pedaled only a few yards away when Kristin started to laugh. "Did you see the look on Kelli's face?" she asked.

"Kris, how *could* you? How could you invite him to dinner right in front of her?"

Kristin backpedaled lazily. "It was the only way to find out. If he hadn't accepted, we'd have known they were a pair. Now at least we know Kelli's crush is one-sided, for the time being. Besides—" she gave me a conspirator's wink. "Things just weren't moving fast enough between you two."

I gulped. It was one thing having Patsy as a boss, but seeing him at *home?*

"Kristin, maybe this isn't such a good idea. I mean, we only met the guy yesterday. Besides, I thought you were the one who thought he was gorgeous."

"I was. I do. But I'll only be here two weeks, and that's not long enough to fall in love, get married, and have six kids. So it's hardly worth it for me to get involved, right?"

"Wrong. Kris, every time you step out your door you fall in love. Remember when you went to Mammoth for two weeks? Or the time you were in Macy's for an *hour?*" I shook my head. "How do you do it? You promise eternal devotion from Minute One, write impassioned love letters for about a week, weep for two hours when it's over, and then

81

it really *is* over. You forget the guy and are in love again by noon the next day. It's bizarre.''

Kristin cocked her head. "Maybe," she said. "But at least I don't need to know a guy's social security number, mother's maiden name, life's goal, and family history back to the year thirteen-oh-two before I decide whether to say 'hello' to him!" Her eyes narrowed. "And I don't stop seeing a guy just when things are starting to get a little bit serious."

I looked away and fiddled with the gearshift on my bike.

"I'm not like you," I said at last. "I mean, it hurts when you get burned. And I don't know if I could handle liking somebody, and then being dumped."

"Uh-huh. So instead of being the dump*ee*, you play the role of the dump*er*."

I braked hard. "What do you mean?"

Kristin doubled-back and stopped. "Face it, Drew. After two or three dates, you throw guys away like Kleenex."

"I do not!"

"I'm not saying you're mean or anything. You always do it nice." Kristin teasingly imitated my voice. " 'I really like you, Poindexter, but I'm not ready to settle down with one guy. I have a lot of fun with you, Zorro, but I need to stay home Saturday nights to wash my hamster.' "

I couldn't help it. I giggled.

"Yeah, but it's not funny, Drew. You never give anyone a chance. And those guys are *nice*. So nice, that they never press to see you again. They just quietly fade into the background. Like Jack."

I didn't say anything. What Kristin said was true.

"Lighten up, kiddo." She punched my bike's horn with a finger. "All I'm saying is, give Patsy a chance. I can tell he likes you. You don't have to get involved or anything. Just spend some time with him. Have some fun. Promise me you'll think about it, okay?"

I sighed. "Okay, Kris. I promise, but—"

"Great!" Without waiting for me to finish my sentence, Kristin pedaled away in a burst of speed, her hair streaming behind her in the wind.

9

I couldn't sleep that night. Couldn't get comfortable. The light touch of sheets against my sunburned shoulders was painful. My face felt as if it could radiate enough heat to melt glaciers.

Your own dumb fault, I scolded myself. I'd spent all day in the sun: first working at the beach shack, then later when Kris and I had ridden our bikes to Koloa for groceries. *Bozo.* Why hadn't I worn a hat and sunscreen?

Wincing, I eased out of bed.

"Where ya goin'?" Kris mumbled.

"Bathroom. Aspirin. Go back to sleep."

"Mmm." She turned over. "G'night."

I groped across the darkened room and opened the door. A light from the bathroom cast a warm yellow glow in the hall.

"Dillon?" The door was open and I poked my head in. Jane stood at the counter, wearing an oversized nightshirt. She was washing something in the sink.

"Oh, Drew! Sorry, did I wake you?"

I shook my head. "I can't sleep. Sunburn. Is there any aspirin?"

"In the medicine cabinet, second shelf." She dried her hands on a towel. "Are you sure I didn't wake you? Marc went back to the clinic to finish some paperwork. I thought I'd wait up for him and take care of a bit of hand laundry at the same time."

"No, really, I didn't hear a thing." I shook two tablets out of the aspirin bottle, then turned to the sink to fill a cup with water. My hand froze in midair. Two round eyes stared up at me from beneath the sudsy water.

"Aakkk!" I jerked back. The tablets clicked to the floor. "What's *in* there?"

Jane laughed. "Don't worry, he won't bite. Just a shark puppet, see?" She plunged her hand in the water and brought up a sodden, dripping creature. I recognized it as one of the stuffed animals I'd seen in Dad's bedroom. The shark was gray with big glass eyes and a stupid grin that revealed white flannel fangs. Jane held it by the dorsal fin.

"Uh, very cute." I bent to hide my smile, pretending to search for the aspirin. "Play with him often?"

"As a matter of fact, yes." Jane dropped the puppet back into the water. "That's why he needs a bath. I use puppets with kids at the clinic. For therapy."

"What kind of therapy?"

"Oh, just to help break the ice. Sometimes it's easier for children to talk through the voice of someone else. Like ol' Mr. Shark here." Jane gave him an affectionate pat. "Sometimes I wish adults could do the same thing. Your dad, for instance. He has a hard time talking about important things. Especially with people he cares about."

"That's not what I heard."

Water gurgled down the drain as Jane began rinsing the puppet. "What do you mean, Drew?"

"Patsy told me he and Dad used to have some long talks."

Jane nodded. "Yes, they got pretty close when Patsy lived here."

"Why *did* he live here?"

"I think Patsy should be the one to tell you that." She gave the puppet a final squeeze. "Let's just say Patsy needed some time away from his own home to make a few decisions, changes. And Marc was there to help him talk things out." She held my gaze for a moment. "You know, I get the feeling you and your dad need to do the same thing."

I shrugged. "We're fine. Really. There's nothing to say." I gulped down my aspirin and headed for the door.

Jane's voice sounded gentle and sad. "Unfortunately, that's exactly what Marc wants to believe."

The next morning I felt irritable. My eyes were puffed and itchy, as if I'd never gone to sleep. The aspirin had helped my sunburn a little, but my conversation with Jane had kept me awake till long after two. I wasn't exactly looking forward to preparing a gourmet meal for Sunglasses that night, either. Dillon was excited about him joining us, and I loved to cook. But every time I thought about Sunglasses and Dad being great buddies I got that empty feeling inside, deep down in a place I could never touch.

Maybe everyone would just forget about the dinner, I thought as Kristin and I pedaled to work.

No such luck.

"I hope you're not planning on eating anything today," Kris said to Sunglasses when we arrived at the shack. "You're gonna want lots of room in that stomach for Drew's coq au vin and my famous chocolate mousse. Both are to *die* for!"

"I'm not eating anything except frustration this morning," Sunglasses replied. He was hunkered down in the grass, several large pieces of posterboard and magic markers scattered around him.

"What are you working on?" I asked.

"Oh—" Sunglasses made a helpless gesture. "Our PR person is on vacation. Management needs me to make a poster for the front lobby advertising the surfing lessons. In the last ten minutes, I've ruined three posters. See? A kindergartener could do better."

"Mmm-hmm," Kristin agreed. "Are those surfboards? Or ironing boards?"

Sunglasses groaned.

"I could make the poster for you," I offered casually, though my fingers itched to get at that lovely expanse of white paper. It'd been so long since I had an idea to work out, a creative challenge to focus on. "I learned a lot at the ad agency I worked for," I added. "I'm pretty good."

"Pretty good?" Kris said. "She's great!"

"That's all I need to know. Okay, Drew, the job's yours. Here." Sunglasses scooped the markers and paper toward me. "I'll pay you extra for the time it takes. Oh, and I need it by tomorrow morning. Think you can do it?"

"I can do it." Suddenly, I didn't feel tired anymore. "I'll have it for you tonight, when you come over for dinner."

"Great. Thank you." He touched my arm. Even after he walked away, I could still feel the warmth from his hand.

Kristin sighed. "It sure would be a lot easier to think of him as just a friend, if he weren't so darn gorgeous!"

I didn't say anything, but I think my arm agreed.

During the next hour, people came in droves to check out towels and chairs. But by ten-thirty the rush had slackened off and Kris decided to go for a swim. That left me free to start work on a few rough sketches.

Designing ads is a little like self-hypnosis. I get so absorbed in the work that all the sights and sounds around me fade away: There's nothing left in the world except the pencil in my hand, the paper on my lap, and the sights and sounds I create in my mind. I was so wrapped up that morning in picturing the way Dillon looked when he surfed, and trying to express that agile energy in a drawing, that I'm not sure how long it took before I realized that someone was watching me.

I dragged my gaze away from the sketches.

Sunglasses lounged in the grass nearby, relaxed back on his elbows. His tanned legs were outstretched, leisurely crossed at the ankles. He looked as if he was content to sit there, watching me, all day.

"How—how long have you been there?" I stammered.

"Awhile. Didn't want to disturb you." He wiggled his nose. "You were making the most outrageous faces."

"I was not!" My cheeks flushed. ". . . was I?"

"Hey, don't be embarrassed. I'm impressed. You

88

love doing that kind of stuff, don't you? The sketches, I mean, not the faces."

Something in his tone made him sound wistful, almost envious. And made me want to share my feelings with him.

"Yeah, I've always loved it," I admitted. "When I was a kid, my mom worked as a commercial artist. She encouraged me to draw and cut pieces of ads out of magazines and glue them to paper, so that I felt like I was helping her. Making ads of my own, you know? In junior high, I started learning more about art and photography, and I realized that I could actually make a career out of something I loved. That's why I took a part-time job at an ad agency. Ads make me feel different inside. I can't pick up a magazine today without analyzing the ads. I try to figure out *how* the colors or lines or words make me feel different. And that helps me learn how to create ads that do the same thing for hundreds, maybe thousands of people."

Sunglasses nodded. "It must feel good to know what you want to do with your life."

"Don't you know? I mean, you could do so much more than—" I stopped.

He snorted. "You mean, 'What's a smart guy like me doing in a place like this'? Well, I'll tell you. I'm surfing. Working. And making a little money. Yeah, it *is* laid-back. But it's my choice. It's something I want to do, *need* to do for now. At least until I decide what I want for the 'after.' "

He tugged at a handful of grass, then let the blades fall through his fingers. "That's one thing your dad taught me. You're responsible for all your decisions. So you've got to make absolutely sure you know what you're doing and what you want.

89

And be honest about it, right from the start. Otherwise you can end up hurting a lot of people. Including yourself.''

''Yes.'' I almost whispered the word. Dad would know that all too well. What had Mom said about him? *''All those years we were married . . . I could tell he was unhappy. But I couldn't get him to admit it, to talk about it.''* But if Dad had known, why didn't he say anything? Didn't he know that the longer he waited, the more pain he'd cause?

I jerked to my feet, spilling markers and pencils onto the grass. ''Oh, Dad's a great one with speeches,'' I said. ''Except when it comes to the people he loves.''

Sunglasses glanced at me in surprise. ''What are you talking about?''

''You don't know, do you?'' My voice sounded cold and even. ''You don't know what my dad did. Well, let me tell you. Two years ago, Dad had to go to a medical convention in Honolulu. He was supposed to be gone four days. Routine, no big deal. Only this time, he packed his bags, kissed Mom, Dillon, and me, waved good-bye, got on the plane and—'' my voice broke ''—and *never came home.''*

Patsy looked as if I had slapped him across the face. His gaze searched mine, as if not quite believing what had happened.

''Drew.'' He reached out and clasped my hand.

I broke away, tears filling my eyes. I wanted to run, but where could I go? There was noplace safe, noplace secure. There were only edges everywhere I turned. . . .

Blindly, I ran into the shack.

Sunglasses followed. Without a word he shut the

door, then put his arms around me. I tried to push away, but he held me tighter.

"It's okay," he whispered, stroking my hair. "It's okay . . ."

A wave of relief broke over me. I clung to him as if he were a lifeline. Then I buried my face in his neck and cried, my salty tears mingling with the sea-salt on his skin.

10

"Hey, what's everyone doin' in here?"

I caught a glimpse of Kristin peering in the door. Sunglasses pointed at her dramatically and said, "Out!"

The door slammed, but not before I saw Kristin smirk.

"Oh, we've really done it now," I said, half-laughing.

"What do you mean?"

"Kristin *invented* the word *gossip.*" I rested my forehead against the soft cotton of his T-shirt. He smelled warm, and faintly of coconut suntan oil. I liked the feeling of his strong arms around me. I didn't ever want to move.

"Are you feeling better?" He stroked my hair again. "Why don't you go on home. Your shift's almost over. Kelli will be here soon. I'll see you tonight, that is, if I'm still invited for dinner."

I leaned back in the circle of his arms. "Of course you're invited. I have to give you the poster, don't I?"

He flashed me such a dazzling smile that I pulled away, embarrassed. I must look awful! Puffy eyes.

Wet, blotchy face. How could he stand to look at me? With the back of my hand I wiped at my eyes and headed back out into the bright sun.

Kristin leaped guiltily away from the door.

"Ready to go?" I asked.

"Uh, sure." She got on her bike while I stuffed the markers into my pack.

"Seven o'clock, right?" Sunglasses called.

"Right. See you." With a wave I pushed off, balancing the posterboard under one arm. *Please let me ride away without falling over,* I thought. My legs felt wobbly. My heart pounded. I knew Sunglasses was watching me.

Kristin and I rode without a word for a few minutes. She kept glancing at me, her expression changing from curious to exasperated.

"So," she began, "read any good books lately?"

"A few."

Silence.

"Um, seen any good movies?"

"No."

Silence.

Kristin jerked her handlebars, almost running me off the road. "Jeez, Drew, aren't you going to say *anything?*"

I laughed. "Kristin, I don't know what you want me to say. Patsy and I were talking about Dad. I started to cry and, well, you saw. It just happened."

"You were talking about your dad?"

"Yeah." I fidgeted with the gearshift, remembering all the times Kristin had tried to discuss the same subject with me, and how I'd always put her off. Maybe if I tried to explain it to her, I could explain it to myself, too.

"Patsy lived with Dad and Dillon for a while," I began. "I don't know why. But he mentioned how much Dad had helped him, and I guess I felt, I don't know—sort of jealous—that Dad would make such an effort with a stranger."

Kristin nodded. "I can understand that."

"Anyway," I went on, "I got angry and blurted out how Dad had deserted us. And I ended up crying in Patsy's arms—that's all."

"But Drew, do you *like* him?"

"Yes," I said. "I like him. A lot." A whole lot, I thought. I didn't know why. But maybe it wasn't important to analyze the whys of liking him. Maybe it was just enough to know that I did.

"I like him, Kristin," I repeated. "And he's coming for dinner, so if your chocolate mousse isn't perfect, I'm gonna mousse your head!"

With a burst of speed, I shot in front of her. For the first time I couldn't wait to get to Dad's house. There was so much to do. Mushrooms to chop, chicken to fry, a poster to design. And I needed a total body make-over. How would I get it all done (especially that last part!) in only seven hours?

Maybe being under pressure helped. By six forty-five the salad was made, the mousse was chilling, and the kitchen smelled warm and tangy with the scent of simmering onions, chicken, and wine. I'd even found a colorful cloth and a set of napkins for the table outside.

"Everything smells and looks wonderful," Jane said when she got home. She stowed her briefcase away, then hurried back into the kitchen, as if afraid she'd miss something if gone too long. "This

94

is high-class, girls,'' she continued. ''Lemon slices in the water glasses. Candles. And Drew! What a great dress!''

''Thanks.'' Kristin had loaned me a cotton-knit sundress. It was the color of cool watermelons, with spaghetti straps, a scoop neck, and low-cut waist. The full skirt swirled just above my knees.

''Seems kinda dumb to do all this just for Patsy,'' Dillon said. He eyed the plumeria I had tucked behind my ear. ''When are we eating, anyway?''

''Soon, I hope,'' Dad said. ''We're starving.'' He stood at the kitchen door, Sunglasses beside him. Sunglasses was dressed casually, wearing a pair of jeans and a faded, blue Hawaiian shirt. But I could tell the shirt had been freshly ironed, and for once, he wasn't wearing his glasses. I'd forgotten how clear and gray his eyes were. Not a cold, steel gray, but as soft and warm as gray flannel.

''I picked these from my garden,'' he said, holding out three yellow rosebuds. ''Three pretty flowers for three pretty women.''

Sunglasses held my gaze until I felt my cheeks ignite. Then I heard Jane say, ''Ooo, flattery will get you—an extra cup of chocolate mousse! Drew, why don't you get a vase from that cupboard. Top shelf. Patsy, let's go outside. I think Drew and Kristin are ready to serve us.''

I was glad that Sunglasses ended up sitting between Dad and Dillon. I wouldn't have been able to eat a thing with his knee touching mine the way Kristin's did at that small table. I was freaked out enough as it was, worrying about the dinner.

''Does the chicken taste okay?'' I asked. ''Anybody want salt? How about more bread? Dillon, do you like that salad dressing? I could get you some Ranch.'' I leapt up from the table and scurried to the kitchen. ''I'm sorry the chicken's not very good,'' I said when I returned. ''I sort of experiment each time I make this, and sometimes it works and sometimes—''

''Will somebody pull her plug?'' Dillon complained.

''Drew, sit down and eat,'' Jane insisted. ''Everything is delicious.''

''If you pick out the mushrooms,'' Dillon mumbled. Jane shot him a sharp glance.

Sunglasses winked at me. I blushed.

''Drew's a perfectionist,'' Dad said with a slow smile. ''Just like her mother. And the Menehunes.''

''Will somebody please tell me who or what are the Menehunes?'' Kristin asked. ''I hear Patsy call Dillon that all the time.''

''The Menehunes are a mythical people,'' Jane said, ''who supposedly lived in the Islands long before the Polynesians.'' She gestured with her fork. ''They were about three feet high, kind of ugly, with big eyes and long eyebrows.''

''Yeah, that's Drew, all right,'' Dillon remarked.

Too bad I wasn't about seven years younger. I would've thrown a mushroom at him.

''Legends say,'' Jane continued, ''that the Menehunes were very industrious, but they only worked at night. If they couldn't finish a project before dawn, they'd quit.''

''That sounds a little like Mom.'' I glanced at Dad. ''Except Mom never quits.''

''I know.'' Dad poked at a chicken wing on his plate. Then he lifted his head, his face brightening.

96

"I remember once, Marlene and I were throwing a huge dinner party. We had maybe thirty people over. V.I.P.'s in the medical profession. Marlene made this same meal. Coq au vin, salad, fancy hors d'oeuvres. Perfect. The whole evening was perfect, until dessert."

"I remember, I remember!" Dillon choked on his laughter.

"Oh, no—" I started to giggle. "You're not going to tell *that* story, are you?"

"What?" Jane asked. "What happened?"

Dad's smile widened. "Marlene made Baked Alaska for dessert. Somehow the curtains caught fire. Smoke started billowing out into the dining room. Then the smoke alarm went off. We all crowded into the kitchen. And there was Marlene, standing on a chair in her evening gown and high heels, whapping the alarm with a broom. She'd gotten the fire out, but everything was black and we had these high ceilings, so she couldn't reach the alarm. We all just stood there with our mouths open, watching her. Marlene whapped the alarm again. It gave a last pathetic beep, and stopped. Then very gracefully, Marlene got down from the chair, still holding the broom, and said, 'Dessert's going to be just a *little* bit late.' "

We all broke up. My stomach ached, but it didn't matter. It felt good. We were all laughing at the dinner table just like a real family.

Except in place of Mom, there was Jane.

Suddenly, I didn't feel like laughing anymore. I stood up, wadding my napkin into a ball.

"I'll get the dessert," I said. My voice came out high and brittle.

Sunglasses moved to help me.

"Thanks." As we walked into the kitchen he took my hand, squeezing it as if in understanding.

"You okay?" he asked.

I squeezed back. "Sure." I took six goblets of mousse and a bowl of whipped cream from the refrigerator.

Sunglasses helped me spoon a dollop of cream in each glass. "This looks fantastic," he said. "I think I'll have to work off all the calories with a long walk. Want to join me?"

"I'd love to, but—"

"But what?"

I dropped an extra puff of cream atop Dillon's mousse, then licked the spoon. "But, I don't think we should go without Kristin."

"No problem," Sunglasses said. "I told Kristin earlier I wanted to talk to you alone."

"And she never said a word!"

"I swore her to secrecy," he whispered into my ear.

After dessert, Sunglasses and I walked hand-in-hand to Poipu Beach. The moon shone on the water, making the foam glow in a magical iridescence. We walked silently, listening to the trade winds rustling the palms.

"Remember what I said earlier," Sunglasses began at last, "about deciding what you want and being honest about it? Right from the start?"

"Yes." The word sounded like a breath.

"Well, what I wanted to say is, I'd really like to spend time with you. More than just at work. And I thought you should know a few things about me, before you decide if you'd like to see me, too."

I released his hand and sat down, burrowing my

feet in the sand to where it still felt warm from the sun. My mind flashed on something Sunglasses had said yesterday. *I've already got a date tonight.*

My heart seemed to deflate. "It's about Kelli, isn't it?"

"Kelli?" Sunglasses sounded confused. "Oh. *Oh.* No, Kelli and I are just friends. We go to a movie now and then, but it's all pretty casual."

Good, I thought, but I didn't say anything.

"I knew I had to tell you this," Sunglasses continued, "after what you said the other day. About me being a loser. You were right. I used to be pretty messed up. When I was going to the university in Honolulu last year, I used a lot of drugs. Not just pot. Cocaine, too. I flunked out of school my first semester. When I went back home to the Big Island, all my parents did was scream at me. Well, my Dad screamed. Mom just cried. So I split. I was eighteen, so I could do what I wanted. I didn't think my parents would care."

Sunglasses was silent for a moment. I glanced over, expecting him to be looking out at the water, or down at his lap. But he was facing me. Gazing right into my eyes, as if it was very important to tell me face on.

He started talking again. He told me about moving to Kauai. How he spent his days surfing and getting high. How he worked at odd jobs, making enough money for drugs and Big Macs. Nights he slept on the floor of a friend's house or on the beach. After a while, he couldn't seem to get high any more. He felt like a whirlpool inside, spiraling downward, lower and lower.

Then one night, feeling lost and alone, he wandered into the Koloa clinic looking for someone, anyone, to talk to.

"That's where I met Jane," Sunglasses said. "We sat in her office all night, talking. I was a mess. Crying. I told her I wanted to kill myself. Jane took me to your dad's house, explained that I needed a place to stay while she counseled me. I lived there three months. Your dad's the one who got me the job at the beach shack. He called my parents, too. Got us to open up a bit. Things aren't perfect between us yet, but the last couple times I called them, my dad and I talked. Really talked. It felt good."

I took Sunglasses' hand again and held it with both of mine. "I'm sorry I called you a loser. Anybody who can come through all that is someone special."

"Yeah, and all that's just my good side."

I knew he was teasing now. Then his voice grew serious again. "Drew, I want you to be honest with me, okay? If the stuff I've been involved in bothers you . . . I mean, I'm straight now, but if you'd rather not spend time with me because of it, or if you have a boyfriend or something, I wish you'd tell me."

"You really want me to be honest?"

He nodded.

"Well, in all honesty—" I stopped. I wanted to tell him that the drug thing didn't matter anymore. That the person he'd become, and the person he had been, were both important to me, because I understood what he'd gone through. I wanted to tell him I knew that spiraling sensation . . . that lost and helpless feeling of plunging downward into nothingness. But words weren't enough. They

100

couldn't express the aching, or the strange, new warmth I felt inside for him.

I moved closer to Sunglasses in the sand and tenderly, kissed him on the cheek.

His eyes glistened. Then he gathered me closer until his soft lips touched mine.

11

Midnight.

I lay on a lounge chair in Dad's front yard, listening to Sunglasses whistle as he strolled barefoot down the driveway. The whistling blended into the hush of warm trades. His shadow disappeared around a bend.

"I only live about a mile from here," he had said, giving me a last kiss—on my nose. But a mile seemed so far away. Almost as far as the next time I'd see him. Tomorrow morning. Nine hours from now. An eternity.

A forgotten beach towel lay under my chair. I pulled it around me, smiling into it as I gazed down at the ocean and the winking lights of condos. I couldn't believe it! Sunglasses and I had been down on the beach for almost three hours. Seemed more like fifteen minutes. We'd kissed for a while, then started talking again. Laughing and interrupting, as if we couldn't share things about ourselves fast enough. I liked to hear Sunglasses talk: about surfing, his favorite books, a silly conversation he'd had once with Dillon. And I liked the breathless feeling I got when his warm lips touched mine.

"Of *course* I'm envious of her. It's only natural."

Jane's voice shattered the balmy quiet. I turned. My chair was only a few feet from Dad's bedroom window. I know I shouldn't have listened. I know I should've gone straight to bed. But I'd never heard Jane sound so angry. Or so desperate.

". . . this is bound to come up again and again," Jane was saying. "She's their mother. And you were married to her for eighteen years. So I know I'm going to hear about her. That's okay. But I get jealous sometimes, like tonight, hearing that story about the dinner party. I think about what she had with you all those years. A family, a real home. And I'm afraid that's a part of you I'll never share."

"I knew I shouldn't have told that story," Dad answered. "I'm sorry, Jane. I won't talk about her again."

"No!" The word sounded like an explosion. "Marc, that's not what I want. I'd *never* ask that of you. It's unrealistic. And unfair. Marc, I love you so much, but sometimes I just want to strangle you! I told you about my jealousy just so you'd know how I feel. I don't want you backing down. Or backing away. Please don't treat me like Marlene. You always gave in to her. You never stood up to her, never fought for what *you* wanted. And she let you get away with it. Well I won't."

A short silence. I held my breath. Then Jane spoke again, her voice low, intense.

"I'm not Marlene, Marc. You can't pull the same thing on me that you did with her. You have to stop being afraid to show your feelings. You have to start being honest with me. I love you. I want a

103

family, a home. But I don't know what *you* want. Start talking to me, Marc, otherwise one day *I'll* be the one who walks away. And you'll feel angry and hurt and resentful for something that's your own damn fault.''

I stood up. I couldn't listen anymore. Didn't want to hear anymore. Something inside me ached for Jane, understood her frustration. Was Dad going to end up hurting her the way he'd hurt Dillon and me? And Mom? At least Jane knew what Dad was like from the start. So far, she had chosen to stay with him, to try and work things out. Dad had never given us that choice.

I hurried into the semidark house, but I'd forgotten to take off my thongs. They made loud slap-slapping sounds on the tiled floor. I whisked them off. Too fast. I lost my balance and stumbled into a chair.

A door opened. A light clicked on. Dad appeared in the living room, wearing pajamas.

''Sorry,'' I whispered. Did he know I'd overheard? I tried to sound innocent. ''I didn't mean to wake you, Dad, but this chair leapt right out at me and—''

''Where have you been?'' Dad demanded.

''With Patsy. Out walking.''

''For three hours? Jane and I've been worried about you. Why didn't you call?''

''From the beach? Dad, we just didn't notice the time. You knew I was with Patsy. What's the big deal?''

''The big deal is—'' Dad's voice trailed off. ''I'm sorry,'' he continued after a moment. ''It's my fault. I never thought to set a curfew for you. From now on, on work nights you'll be in by eleven. Weekends, I think midnight is fair.''

I stared at him. "No way. At home, Mom lets me stay out until one.''

"Well, I'm your father and I say midnight.''

"What is this sudden 'Daddy Authority' stuff?'' I said. "You haven't been too worried about me the last couple of years, so why bother now?''

"Please don't shout.''

Don't shout? I wanted to scream at him, but that familiar dizzy sensation whirled inside me. I clung to the chair to keep from falling.

Dad reached toward me. "Drew—?''

"Leave me alone!'' I jerked back. "I'm all right.''

As if walking a tightrope, I backed away, afraid I'd topple over any second. "I'll obey your rules,'' I said, my words sounding numb. "I'll be in by twelve. I'll call to let you know where I am. But I'm not doing it because of you. I'm doing it because this is your house, and I want to stay here to see Dillon. That's all. That's *all.*''

I stumbled down the hall to my bedroom.

"Drew?'' Kristin's voice was a tentative whisper.

"Yeah.'' I leaned against the door, my palms spread flat on the wood. *Breathe deeply*, I thought. *That's it. One, two.*

"Drew, are you okay? I couldn't help overhearing—''

"I'm okay, Kris. Thanks.'' I undressed, moving as if balancing something fragile on my head. In the moonlight I could see Kristin, propped on one elbow. I got into bed beside her. We were silent for several minutes.

105

"Well, uh, how was your walk?" she finally asked.

My anger began to drain away. I sighed at the ceiling. "He's wonderful, Kris. The whole night was wonderful. He calls me *kuuipo*. That's Hawaiian for 'my sweetheart.' "

I heard a rustle of sheets. Kristin touched my arm. "Are you going to see him again?"

"He wants to take me out tomorrow night," I said. "And Thursday night and Friday night and sight-seeing on Saturday . . . but I said no."

"You *what?!*"

"Kristin, you're my guest. I can't desert you like that."

"Desert me, desert me! I don't mind. Well, maybe just a little."

"No, I can go out with him after you leave."

Kristin jerked upright. "No way, José! I know you, Drew. If you put this relationship on hold for even a *second,* you'll come up with some ridiculous reason for never seeing Patsy again. Uh-uh. I don't want that to happen. Look, go out with him tomorrow night. Then see if he has a cute friend for me, and we'll double the next night. And take me sight-seeing with you on Saturday, okay?"

I sighed with relief. I hadn't really wanted to wait two weeks to out with Sunglasses again. Yet I hadn't wanted to be unfair to Kristin, either. "That would be great, Kris. Are you *sure* you don't mind?"

Kristin flipped her hair over one shoulder. "Of course not. It'll be so neat watching you two happen! Besides, I'm reading a wonderfully trashy romance novel, so as long as I have my book for the nights and you for the days, everything's cool."

106

I leaned over and gave her an awkward hug. Then, feeling as if that wasn't enough, I got out of bed and took something down from the window-sill.

"What are you doing?" Kris whispered.

"Getting this." I placed it in her hand.

"What—?" she began. "Oh, it's the trophy I gave you. But that was for your flight. Why are you giving it back to me?"

"Read it," I said.

"I don't have to read it. I bought it, remember? It says THE BEST."

"And that's what you are. The best friend I ever had." I slid back into bed. "Thanks for always being here for me, Kris. I know I'm a real pain sometimes."

She didn't answer. After a while, she started singing an old sappy song about friendship from our Girl Scout days.

I joined in and we warbled off-key. We sounded so awful that we both started to giggle. The giggles turned to laughter, which we couldn't stop because we knew we *should*. We might wake up Dad and Jane. Or worse, Dad might think I was laughing about our quarrel. We put our hands over our mouths. It was like trying to stop a sneeze. The laughs came out in convulsive, choking sounds. Every time we'd stop, we'd glance at each other and crack up all over again. We laughed until we were exhausted, tears running down our cheeks, our stomachs weak and achy.

"Good night, you bozo," Kristin said sleepily, when at last we calmed down.

"Good night." I lay awake for a long time, listening to her slow, even breaths. I'd never have a better friend. She was great, always knowing when to make me laugh. And always knowing when laughter just wasn't enough.

The next few days passed quickly. Mornings, Kristin and I worked at the beach shack. Afternoons we spent doing one or more of the four S's: sunbathing, snorkeling, swimming, and Kris's favorite, shopping. Nights were best of all. I spent every second of them with Sunglasses.

One evening we went to the movies and then dancing. The next night, Sunglasses got a date for Kristin, and the four of us ate dinner at an elegant restaurant overlooking the water.

The third night was the most romantic. We packed a picnic supper, borrowed Dad's bikes, and took a moonlit ride along an old road that paralleled the beach. Our slanted shadows flickered on the street, making us look like figures in an old-time movie. We stopped, finally, to rest, feeding each other chicken legs and papaya slices. We hugged and laughed and talked. Then Sunglasses told me several ancient Hawaiian legends he'd heard from Jane. I'm not sure which glittered more: the moon on the water or the enchantment in his eyes. I could've sat there, listening to him all night. But I made sure we were home by eleven. I wanted no more confrontations with Dad.

Not that I had to worry about that. By Saturday, I hadn't seen Dad in three days. He was always gone in the mornings before seven and didn't get home from work until after Kris and I were in bed. Jane said he was working double shifts at the clinic. Patient backlog or something. Her voice had been calm, casual when she'd said it, but I noticed her hand trembling a little as she reached for her coffee mug.

"Hey, great news," Sunglasses said when he arrived at the house early Saturday morning. He jangled the keys Jane tossed him for her Subaru. Since he didn't own a car, Jane had agreed to let us borrow hers for our sight-seeing tour.

"Let me guess," Kristin said. "You found an actual Menehune to take us sight-seeing. Only one problem: We have to go in the dead of night."

"Wrong!" Sunglasses flashed his smile my way. "Management loved your surfing poster, Drew. In fact, they want you to design their new restaurant menus."

"You're kidding!"

"Nope. You meet with them next week. They're paying fifteen dollars an hour, so make it a looong menu!"

"Oh, Patsy, thank you!"

I threw my arms around him. We hugged for a long time. Then he kissed me and murmured, "You know, *kuuipo,* I kinda like the sound of that."

"Sound of what?" I asked, confused.

"My name. That's the first time you've called me by my name."

"Oh, well—" Embarrassed, I glanced down at my feet. I didn't know what to say. How could I, when I didn't know myself why I'd still been calling him Sunglasses?

"Come *on,* you guys," Kristin called from the backseat of the car. "There are about three thousand places I want to see before noon. Oh, and can we stop and buy postcards someplace first?"

109

Patsy started the car. "Your wish is my command!"

I couldn't remember ever having a more perfect day. We started the morning eating banana-macadamia-nut pancakes at a funky little café in Lihue. Then we drove to the North Shore, stopping to see Wailua Falls, Kilauea Lighthouse, a large cave called the Fern Grotto, and miles and miles of golden beaches.

Kris tirelessly snapped pictures of everything. It wasn't until we stood overlooking the green patchwork valley of Hanalei that someone finally took a picture of *her*. When her sundress billowed around her waist in a sudden gust of wind, a group of male Japanese tourists aimed their cameras her way. Their shutters clicking, they bowed with bright grins and chorused in clipped English: "Oh, thank you, thank you very much!"

Kristin only laughed. "Do you think I should give them my autograph?"

Later, on the way home, Kristin snoozed in the backseat like a contented cat. She slept so soundly that Patsy and I didn't bother to wake her when we got out of the car to take pictures of the Menehune Fish Pond.

"Think she had fun?" Patsy asked me, gesturing at the backseat.

I put my arms around him and rested my head on his chest. "I know she did. I did too. Thanks, Pats, it was a perfect day. You and Kristin and Dillon have really made this trip to Hawaii worthwhile."

"I'm sure it's been nice to see your dad, too."

I felt myself stiffen. "Not especially."

Patsy sighed. "Look, Drew, it's obvious you

110

guys aren't on the best of terms, but he *is* your dad. You might not always agree on stuff, but there's a bond there, you know?''

''Not anymore there isn't, so don't push me, all right?'' I pulled away from him and pretended to focus the camera slung across my shoulder.

''How long are you gonna keep punishing him?'' Patsy continued. ''It's been two years since the divorce. I just don't understand why you haven't made up. He cares so much about you. I know, because we've talked. It seems to me that if you'd just reach out—''

I didn't hear the rest of Patsy's sentence. Instead, his words of the other day echoed in my mind. *''I got pretty close to Dillon and your dad . . . they helped a lot. Especially your dad. We had some good talks.''*

Anger and jealousy flared inside me. And yet, looking at Patsy, I also felt a part of me start to freeze over.

''Couldn't you try, Drew?'' he asked. ''It was hard for me to open up at first about my problems, but then—''

''You still don't get it, do you?'' I said, my words coming hot and fast. ''You don't understand what my dad did, what my dad *is*. You think he's wonderful. A sweet doctor who stitches up your surf buddies for free, who talks to you about your life, your choices, your dreams. Well, he's not so wonderful. He's a cold, heartless man who deserted his family without so much as one spoken word. He just dropped bombs. Letter bombs. *Wham!* I'm never coming home. *Wham!* I don't love your mother anymore. *Wham! Wham!* Take that, and that!''

111

Patsy grabbed my arms. "But, Drew, maybe your dad has changed."

"I couldn't care less, Patsy, don't you see? I have nothing to say to him. Please let me go."

Patsy's grasp tightened. "But, Drew, listen—"

"I said, let me go!" I broke free of his grasp. Then I threw myself into the car and slammed the door. Patsy got in on his side and slammed his door, too. We glared at each other.

"What's going on?" Kristin mumbled from the depths of the backseat.

I didn't say anything. Just stared out the window. I tried to control my breathing. It felt like my chest was going to explode.

"Nothing's going on," Patsy said, his words tight, clipped. "We're going home." He started the car, gunning the engine, and threw it into gear. "We'll talk about this later, Drew," he added.

"Sure," I said with a shrug, but I knew I was lying. It was over, Patsy and me, over before it had even really started. It had to be, because no matter how much I liked Patsy, no matter how nice, how kind, how devastatingly cute I thought he was, nothing could ever develop between us. Because Dad was between us. Because Patsy *liked* Dad.

12

"What was all that about in the car?" Kristin demanded when we were home, alone, in our room.

"What was all *what* about?" I flopped across the bed and started flipping through a magazine.

"The big silent treatment between you and Pats. The tension you could cut with a knife." Kristin kneeled on the floor in front of me, chin resting on the bedspread, our noses almost touching. "You're doing it again, aren't you?" she said, staring right into my eyes.

I stared back. "Doing what?"

"Playing the dumper. Patsy's out the door, isn't he? You're gonna tell him to take a hike. Hit the trail. Vamoose. Skidaddle. Game over. Am I right?"

I sat up, tossing the magazine aside. "It wasn't working out, Kris."

"I thought for *once* you were gonna give a guy a chance!" Kristin threw up her hands. "Oh, I know you think you did. Sure. You went out with him five times before dumping him, instead of the usual two or three. Big effort, Drew."

113

I felt a hard lump in my throat. "I tried, Kristin. Believe me, this time I really did try."

"Yeah, I know. And you seemed pretty happy for a while, too." A sigh. "So what are you gonna tell him? That you need time to think? That you're not ready for anything serious?"

"Well, and you only have a week of vacation left, Kris. I want to spend that time together."

"Oh, no. You're not going to use *me* as an excuse. Forget it!" She lay down next to me on the bed and stared up at the ceiling. "You're nuts. Crazy," she said, her tone softening. "Absolutely certifiable. Patsy's the best thing that's ever happened to you, Drew. Don't you *know* that?"

"I don't know anything anymore."

With that, I left the room, mumbling something about helping Jane with dinner. I kept myself busy, kept myself from thinking by scrubbing potatoes and setting the table. Yet an element of truth in Kristin's words kept niggling at the back of my mind all the rest of that evening.

On Sunday, Patsy called.

"I want to talk to you," he said. "Could I come over around noon? Or this evening?"

"I don't think that's a very good idea." My stomach quivered as I spoke.

"Which isn't a good idea? The times . . . or talking to me?"

"Both. I told you yesterday that I had nothing to say when it comes to my dad, so let's just drop it, all right?"

"No, it's not all right," Patsy insisted. "Look, I really enjoy spending time with you. But if this

114

relationship is going to lead anywhere, we've got to talk.''

I shook my head, even though I knew he couldn't see me. ''Patsy, I've been thinking, and, well—'' I took the plunge ''—I think we should stop seeing each other.''

He drew a quick breath. ''Drew. I can't believe you're doing this.''

''Well, you're my boss,'' I went on, ''and it's sort of improper for us to date, considering your other employees and all. But I'll still see you at work.''

''Oh, I'm vastly relieved to hear that,'' Patsy said with a bitter laugh. Then his voice grew soft. ''Drew, I know I upset you yesterday, and I'm sorry. But to end things so abruptly just because—''

I cut him off. ''Patsy, things have been happening too fast between us. I think it's better if we cool off for a while. I gotta go now. Dillon's calling me. I'll see you tomorrow at work.''

Before he could reply, I hung up.

There. It was over. Now I could get on with my life, the way my life was supposed to be. Safe. Easy. With no silly attachments to mess things up. Sure, Patsy and I had fun together. But it didn't matter. *He* didn't matter.

And yet, long after I'd disconnected, I kept my hand on the receiver, as if somehow, someway, I might still be linked to Patsy on the other end. . . .

''Fold these towels. Put them in that bin. When you're finished, hose down those chairs. And it wouldn't hurt to fake a smile now and then. You're scaring the guests.''

That's the way Patsy had talked to me for three

115

days: cold, uncaring, almost rude. Gone was the easy teasing, the secret winks, the quick hugs behind the shack. It hurt to have him act this way, but wasn't that what I had wanted?

"No, not that one!" he shouted. He grabbed the towel I'd just placed in one bin and threw it into another.

"That's the bin you pointed to," I snapped.

"No it isn't. Pay attention."

I bit back my anger and refolded the towel.

Two ten-year-olds scampered up, breathless, excited, and decked out in brand-new surf trunks.

Patsy flashed a grand smile. "Hey, kids!" he said. "Ready for your surf lessons? Okay, go behind the shack and choose your boards. I'll be with you in a second." He turned back to me, the smile wiped clean.

"What do you want me to do when I finish the chairs?" I asked coolly.

"I don't care." He hefted his surfboard and sauntered off with the kids.

I flung the towel I was holding into the bin with a violence that surprised me. Fine. So he didn't care. That made things so much easier. Mentally I flung the last remnants of my feelings for him into the bin, too.

Patsy stayed in the water almost the whole morning. I wondered if he had a full schedule, or if he just didn't want to be near me. Well, I didn't want to be near him either. I hoped he'd stay out until I left work at noon.

No such luck. He wandered back just as I finished folding the final pile of towels inside the shack.

"I'm leaving now," I said. "Anything else you need done?"

He shook his head, then just stood there in the doorway for a long minute, as if debating whether to say something. He must not have liked my expression, because his mouth tucked down, and he turned away.

I felt a pang inside that I knew was a reflection of the hurt I'd seen on his face. I tried to shrug it off. Patsy would be okay, I thought. He'd get over me. He still had Dad and Dillon. Surfing. And Kelli. Soon she'd come trilling back on the scene, looking so cute and breathless in her ruffled bikini that Patsy would wonder why he'd ever thought of her as just a friend.

On Thursday, I awoke to the sound of rain hammering on the roof. Kristin crept deeper under the covers. I envied her. If the rain didn't let up, there wouldn't be much work to do at the shack, and I might be able to avoid a day with Patsy and come back to bed. But first I had to at least make an appearance.

"Here, take the truck," Jane offered, tossing me a set of keys at breakfast. "You'll get drenched, otherwise. Your dad and I will ride together to the clinic."

"Okay, thanks," I answered, and hurried off to the shack.

To my amazement, a few minutes after reaching Kapakai, the downpour stopped. The once-deserted beach now blossomed with tourists and towels, like flowers after a rain. Not too many people ventured near the water, though. The normally calm, aqua-colored surf had changed to a stormy steel blue.

117

Wild waves flung themselves violently against the shore.

"I can't believe he's out in this rough water," Patsy murmured under his breath a couple of hours later. His words surprised me for a second. It was probably the longest sentence either one of us had uttered to each other all morning.

I glanced at him, then followed his gaze. He had stopped working on the inventory and was shielding his eyes, squinting out toward the water.

"Who are you talking about?" I asked.

"That little know-it-all. Phil. I gave him his first surf lesson yesterday, and already he thinks he's Tommy Curren." I followed Patsy as he moved closer to the beach, motioning for the kid to come in.

The kid misunderstood, and waved.

"Damn, he's not paying attention!" Patsy cupped his hands around his mouth. "Phil!" he shouted. "Outside!"

"What's that mean?" I asked.

"It means there's a large wave coming," Patsy said impatiently, "and it's going to break *outside* of where they usually do. If Phil doesn't start paddling quick, he'll end up under it."

"Oh, no."

I watched as the wave grew like a wild animal, rearing its head.

Patsy shouted again. Turning, the kid finally spotted the wave. He started to paddle. Faster. Too late. The wave broke, a wall of water and foam thundering down on top of him.

I held my breath. Counted the half seconds with my heartbeats. *Where are you?* I thought. *You're*

just a kid. Maybe somebody's brother. Like Dil-
lon . . .

A surfboard bounced to the surface and floated toward shore.

No rider.

Shouting, several people raced into the water. Patsy dropped his clipboard and flew after them, his arms pumping, legs almost a blur. And then, he stumbled. I saw it happen in slow motion. One minute he was running. The next, floating down, down, eternal seconds ticking as his body plunged awkwardly, headfirst into the water. Then a wave broke over him.

My heart skidded. Patsy didn't come up. I imagined him being tossed about, submerged under pounds of water, struggling for air, fighting, falling, helpless. . . .

I ran down the beach, barely feeling the hot, burning sand under my feet. People around me shouted that Phil had been rescued, but I didn't care. I thrashed into the surf, up to my knees, my waist . . .

"Patsy!"

He bobbed to the surface a few feet away. I splashed toward him and grabbed his arm. I almost laughed with relief, until I saw the gash on his temple. Blood poured down his face. It shimmered an obscene red.

"Patsy."

He staggered, and I put my arms around his wet body. He coughed up a mouthful of water. "I can't believe this is happening to me," he said through clenched teeth. "I tripped over a stupid rock."

"Oh, God, Patsy," I said. My voice sounded hoarse with emotion. "Patsy, I thought . . . I

119

thought you'd *drowned.*" I swallowed the fear still rising in my throat. "Come on, you've gotta get back to shore."

"I—I'll need your help, Drew. I feel sorta dizzy."

"Okay." I draped Patsy's arm across my shoulder, letting him lean against me. A tourist must've seen us struggling through the tugging waves, because suddenly he was beside us, reaching for Patsy's other arm. Together we half-carried Patsy up the beach and out to the parking lot. While the tourist eased Patsy into the truck, I ran back to the shack.

"What's going on?" Kelli asked, just arriving for work.

"Patsy's hurt. We're going to the hospital." I grabbed several towels from the bin. "Take over, Kelli. I'll call you later." Without waiting for a response, I raced back to the truck.

Patsy had his eyes closed, his head resting against the passenger-door window. I slid in beside him and tucked two towels around his body to keep him warm. Then I looked at his forehead. He had an awful gash, maybe two inches long. My stomach twisted. I glanced away. Took a deep breath. Then, gently, I placed a third towel against the wound.

Patsy winced.

"I know, I know," I murmured. "Here, hold this towel just like this. That's good."

"Thanks."

I started the engine. "Okay, we're going. How do I get to the hospital?"

"No, not there," Patsy said as the truck jostled

toward the exit. "Take me to the clinic. It's closer. And I don't trust anyone except your dad."

"Uh-uh. You're going to the emergency room at the hospital."

"Drew, I can't afford the hospital. Take me to the clinic."

We hit a sudden bump. Patsy grimaced and let out a moan.

"Okay, the clinic!"

I down-shifted swiftly, the gears protesting, and shot out to the main road.

We reached the clinic in Koloa fifteen minutes later. It was a small building, nestled beside a large banyan tree. I zipped into the nearest parking space and yanked on the brake.

"Wait here," I said to Patsy, as I leapt out the door.

"I can make it in," he argued. "Just let me lean on you—"

"I said *wait.*"

"Yes, ma'am!" He saluted me, then mustered a smile. I hurried inside.

The waiting room looked similar to my dentist's office at home. A few chairs. Several people leafed through magazines. An aquarium bubbled soothingly in the corner. The air smelled of antiseptic and plastic.

"I need to see Dr. Mueller right away," I said to the nurse sitting at the reception desk.

She handed me a clipboard. "I'm sorry, miss, he's with a patient right now. He'll be able to see you in a few minutes. Now if you'll just fill out this form—"

"No, you don't understand. This is an emergency."

The nurse reached for her phone. "Let me call one of the other doctors for you."

Again, frustration edged my voice. I drummed my fingers on the desk. "Listen, I'm Drew Mueller. Dr. Mueller is my father. Will you *please* tell him I have to see him right away. It's very important."

The word *father* must've clicked. Quickly, the nurse punched three buttons and murmured something into the phone. Within a minute, Dad sailed into the waiting room, his stethoscope hanging lopsidedly around his neck. There were dark circles under his eyes. He looked tired and frightened.

"Sweetheart, are you all right?" He reached for my arm. "What's happened?"

"It's Patsy, Dad. He cut his head on a rock. Looks pretty bad."

"Where is he now?"

"Outside. In your truck."

"Okay," Dad said. "Don't worry, we'll take care of him." He breathed a sigh, eyes closed for a moment, then gave my arm a reassuring squeeze. "Kim, could I have a wheelchair, please? Drew, wait here."

He wheeled in Patsy a couple of minutes later.

"You really should've gone to the hospital for this," Dad said.

Patsy shifted uncomfortably in the chair. He looked, for a second, small and vulnerable. "Yeah," he answered, "but you're cheaper, aren't you, Marc?"

Dad laughed. "Just remember, you get what you pay for. Okay, Pats. I'm going to send you down the hall to get that cut cleaned up. I'll be back to stitch it in a little while. Drew, would you to wait in my office? Kim will show you the way.''

Dad disappeared down the hall. I followed the nurse to a small room off the reception area. There were diplomas and certificates hanging on one wall, a bookcase crammed with medical texts along another. On the paper-littered desk, I noticed an old framed portrait of Dillon and me.

I glanced away, feeling as if someone had squeezed my heart.

''Just have a seat anywhere,'' Kim said, smiling. She slipped out again in her silent, white shoes, leaving the door ajar, leaving me alone.

13

I paced for several seconds, not really sure what to do with myself, then sat in an armchair. I bit my nails. Tapped my foot. I felt tense inside, as if I was guarding myself against being tickled. And images of Patsy kept replaying in my mind. Patsy tumbling through the air. Patsy being swallowed by the wave. And blood . . . blood on Patsy's face.

Think of something else, I told myself.

Voices drifted down the hall. An elderly voice, frightened, questioning. And Dad's: soothing, reassuring. For the next hour, I concentrated only on the voices, listening to Dad greet each new patient in this same careful, caring way. The people always responded with trust. With hope. They *liked* him. How different this all was from the crazy, hectic practice Dad had run in San Francisco. How different Dad was. So at ease, so *happy.*

Eventually, the voices stopped. Another hour passed. I fidgeted in my seat. What was taking so long? Could something be seriously wrong with Patsy?

"I'm okay," he said, when at last Dad wheeled him into the office. He didn't look too okay. His face was pale, haggard. A wide, white bandage covered the gash on his temple.

"Couple of weeks, and you'll be good as new," Dad pronounced. "No surfing, of course. Just take it easy. Give those stitches a chance to heal."

Patsy forced a grin. "You got it."

"Good. Drew can take you home now. Oh, and you might need these painkillers for a few days." Dad took a small bottle out of his pocket and tossed it into Patsy's lap. "Go easy on them."

"You know I will. Thanks, Marc."

Dad squeezed Patsy's shoulder, then glanced at me.

"Thank you," I said, meaning it.

He looked as if about to say something, then just nodded and left the room.

I wheeled Patsy to the truck and helped him into the passenger seat. As I pulled out of the parking lot, an uneasy silence grew between us.

"Are you sure you want to drive me home?" Patsy asked. "If one of my employees saw us, they might think something's fishy."

"I don't mind," I answered.

"No. Really. Our reputations are at stake here. How about if I call a cab?"

"That won't be necessary."

"Think it over. Things could happen pretty fast between us in here, even if I do have twenty stitches in my head."

I glanced at Patsy, my face flushing. "Do you mind if we talk about something else?"

"Yes, I do mind. Pull over for a second."

"Why?"

"Please. Just do it."

125

"Oh, all right." I maneuvered the car off the road and under the shade of a large tree.

"What?" I said, facing him.

He smiled. "You can drop the pose, Drew."

"What pose?"

"The I-don't-care-about-you-one-bit pose. I saw your face when you 'rescued' me. And a few minutes ago, in your dad's office. There was a lot more caring in your expression than I'd ever see in *any* of my employees." He reached over and grabbed my hand. "You like me and you like me a lot. Admit it."

At Patsy's touch, I felt those familiar tingles start to creep up my arm.

"Yes, I like you," I whispered, looking away. "And that's the problem."

"What's the problem? Drew, look at me." He tugged on my hand. "Are you scared of getting hurt? Because I swear, I will never intentionally do anything to hurt you. Are you scared of things happening too fast? Fine, we'll move slow, at whatever pace makes you comfortable. Drew, you are so important to me that I'm willing to do almost anything to make this work. But we have to talk things out. We have to *try.*"

"I don't know, Patsy."

"Drew, I'm not asking you to marry me. Just go to the movies, out to dinner now and then. Anything you want. How often or infrequent you want. But please hang in there. Give us a try, okay?"

"Well . . ." I paused. "Okay."

He chuckled. "Try to contain your enthusiasm."

"Patsy, I said okay."

He reached over and took my other hand. "Not

good enough. I want to hear you shout gleefully, *Okay! Okay!*"

"Okay! Okay!" I repeated, laughing.

Patsy grinned. "Great. Now will you marry me?"

"Oh, *you!*" I gave him a little shove.

"Ouch. Watch it, I'm an invalid, remember? And I need lots of T.L.C. Come here." He eased me into his arms. We hugged awkwardly. The front seat was cramped, but it didn't matter. It only mattered that his fingers were tracing my shoulder, that I could rub my face against his rough cheek.

We kissed for a while. Then I edged back a little, not because I didn't want to kiss him, but because I wanted to be able to see him, to look into his eyes, to touch his face now and then in wonder, reassuring myself that he was there, that I hadn't pushed him away with our fight, with my cold words. . . .

"I've missed you so much," he murmured into my hair.

"Me too." We hugged some more. He played with my fingers. I rested my head against his chest, listening to the steady thud of his heart. The afternoon deepened around us. A breeze flirted with his hair, tickled my cheek.

At last, I pulled away. "I'd better get you home," I said, starting the engine.

Patsy smiled. "To be continued."

We drove a couple of miles in silence. "You're awfully quiet," he commented. "What are you thinking about?"

I sighed. "Nothing."

"Come on, Drew. We're on a roll here, so fess up. Is something bothering you?"

127

"No. Yes. Well, I was just thinking about Dad."

"What about him?"

"I saw a different side of him today. While waiting for you, I overheard him talking to his patients at the clinic. He sounded so . . . caring. Loving. As if each one of them were a member of his family."

"He's supposed to sound like that," Patsy said. "It's called a bedside manner. Doctors major in it their first year in medical school, taking classes like Empathy 101, and Sympathetic Noises 304."

I had to smile. "I know, Patsy. It's just—I don't understand. How can Dad act that way with total strangers, and yet so unfeeling toward his own family? It doesn't seem possible that the man I saw at the clinic is the same man who . . . who wrote me that letter two years ago." My throat ached. I flicked on the radio, jabbing at the station selectors. Rock music filled the cab.

Patsy snapped off the radio. "Drew," he began, "Drew, as long as we're clearing the air . . . what *was* in that letter?"

"Nothing," I said. "That's the problem. He really said . . . nothing." I tapped my finger against the steering wheel. "Are we getting close to your place? You didn't give me directions."

"Turn right up there," Patsy said. "Go about half a mile, then left at the lava gate. I live in the caretaker's cottage."

I followed his instructions, driving through the gates and up the grass driveway of a beachfront estate. I parked in front of a tiny building. It was about the size of Dad's living room, set back away from the main house.

I helped Patsy out of the truck and up the two

steps of his porch. As he fumbled for his keys, I said, "Patsy, would you like to read my dad's letter?"

"If you want me to. You mean you have it with you?"

I pointed to the car. "It's in my pack. In my wallet. I—I always carry it with me."

"Oh." He leaned against the door. "Have you ever shown it to anyone else? Kristin, your mom, or—"

I shook my head.

"Then why me?" he asked.

"I don't know." I stared down at the wood slats of the porch. "Maybe because . . . because you two get along so well. Maybe you can help me make some sense of it all."

"Okay, Drew." He kissed my cheek. "If you're really sure."

I took a deep breath. "I'm sure."

14

I got Patsy settled on his saggy couch with a 7-Up and a painkiller. Then I called Kristin and told her about the accident.

"I'm gonna spend the afternoon and evening here with Pats," I told her. "Tell Jane I won't be home for dinner."

"Waitaminutedon'tyoudarehangup!" Kristin's voice rose an octave. "Does this mean you two are back together?"

"Mmmmm, maybe."

"You are! I knew it! Okay, hang up, hang up. You can talk to me anytime. But later, we've got a date. I want to hear *details!*"

I laughed. "Right. See you tonight. Oh, and if Dillon's home, would you put him on a minute?"

"Sure."

Dillon sounded anxious when he got on the line. "Is Patsy okay?" he asked. "Does he need anything? I could bring him some books, or go to the store for him on my bike or—"

"Whoa there, Dill Pickle," I interrupted. "I'm sure you'll be the first person Pats will call if he needs anything. Now listen, I just wanted to warn

130

you. The water's pretty rough today, so be careful if you go out surfing.''

Dillon gave a snort of disgust. "Man, what are you, my mother or something?''

"No. It's just that there was this kid today, the one Patsy was trying to save. He wiped out, and he didn't come up for air for the longest time, and . . . and I thought of you, and—''

It was Dillon's turn to interrupt. "Hey, Sis, I'm not a kid anymore, remember? I know how to take care of myself.''

I smiled into the phone. Dillon sounded so, well, adult. Sure of himself. Guess he wasn't doing too badly in Hawaii, after all. "Yeah, okay, Dill,'' I said. "See you later.''

Next I dialed the number for the beach shack so Patsy could fill in Kelli about his injury. While he talked, I took a minute—and that's all it took—to look around his place.

The house had faded, moss green linoleum floors, with a few woven mats spread here and there. The living room was furnished with the couch, a lopsided coffee table, a row of book-shelves stuffed with paperbacks, a cassette deck, and three surfboards leaning against the far wall. To the right, long strands of tiny seashells hung from ceiling to floor as a partition leading into the bedroom. Patsy had a double bed and more book-shelves, this time stuffed with T-shirts and shoes. There were surf posters tacked on the walls. To the left of the living room was a matchbox-sized kitchen, and an even smaller bathroom, complete with mold-encrusted shower.

"Quite a palace, huh?'' Patsy asked, as he hung up the phone.

"Well, at least it has a nice view." The sliding screen doors faced a velvety lawn that sloped to a gold-sand cove.

"The rent is cheap, too." Patsy took a swallow of soda. "I get all this free, in exchange for doing yard maintenance for the estate. I have my own private beach, too. We'll go for a swim there, as soon as my head is better."

I perched on the edge of the couch, trying not to jiggle him. "Can I get you anything else? A pillow, something to eat?"

Patsy shook his head.

"Well, um. Guess I'll get the letter."

I got my pack from the truck. Back in the living room, I unzipped the secret flap of my wallet and handed Patsy a small folded envelope. Then I sat cross-legged on a mat, several feet away. I heard the rustling of paper as he opened the letter.

I shut my eyes. I could see it perfectly in my mind. Cream-colored paper, with a tiny hotel logo in the right-hand corner. Below that, Dad's handwriting: small, neat, angular.

DEAR DREW:

I DON'T QUITE KNOW HOW TO TELL YOU THIS. I GUESS STRAIGHT OUT IS THE BEST WAY.

WHEN THE MEDICAL CONVENTION IS OVER THIS WEEK, I'LL BE STAYING IN HAWAII PERMANENTLY. AFTER A LOT OF CAREFUL THOUGHT, I'VE REALIZED MY PLACE IS NO LONGER IN SAN FRANCISCO. MY PLACE IS NO LONGER BESIDE YOUR MOTHER.

AS SOON AS I'M SETTLED, I'LL SEND YOU MY ADDRESS. I HOPE YOU'LL WRITE TO ME, LET

ME KNOW HOW YOU'RE FEELING. I'M GOING
TO MISS YOU VERY MUCH.

   LOVE,

     DAD

"Was that *all?*"

"That was all." I looked at Patsy. He frowned.

"What happened after that?" he asked.

"Dillon got a similar letter," I said. "So did
Mom. Dad told her he didn't love her anymore.
That he hadn't for a long time. She didn't believe
it at first. She thought he'd be back. He'd been born
in Honolulu. My Grandpa Joe was stationed there
during World War Two. So Mom figured Dad was
just tired of San Francisco. Wanted to get back to
nature for a while. He'd always been more 'earthy'
than she." I plucked a piece of straw from the floor
mat, rolling it between my fingers. "But then a
month later, Mom got another letter, from an at-
torney. Dad had filed for divorce."

Patsy gave a low whistle. "How did your mom
take it?"

"Not too well." My voice sounded hoarse. "She
cried for a solid week. Some days, she wouldn't
even get out of bed. Or else she'd wander around
the apartment in her old bathrobe, not talking, not
eating."

"Scary," Patsy said.

I nodded. "I didn't know what to do. I was only
fourteen, and suddenly I had to take charge. Cook
for Dillon, get him ready for school. Then, one
day, Mom kinda snapped out of it. After that, she
buried herself in her art gallery, working later,
traveling a lot."

"And Dillon?"

133

"Typical Dill." I almost smiled. "When he read Dad's letter, he got real pissed. Screamed, shouted, threw things. Then he seemed okay. When Dad called a few months later, to see if either of us wanted to live with him, Dillon jumped at the chance. Mom objected, at first. She was afraid that if Dad could desert us kids once, maybe he'd do it again. And after losing Dad, I think she was afraid maybe she'd never see Dillon again."

"But Dillon's here."

"Oh, yeah. Dill finally wore Mom down. She told me holding him back would only make him hate her. Hate us. He wanted to go *so* badly."

"Did you ever talk to Dillon about it?" Patsy asked. "Why he made such an about-face? And why it was so important for him to go?"

"Oh, I tried," I said. "But you know how kids are. He just kept saying, 'I want to, Drew. I *have* to.' It was almost as if Dillon wanted to be a kind of watchdog. Always by Dad's side, guarding him so he'd never get another chance to leave . . ."

"And what about you, Drew?" Patsy asked. "What did you say to your dad about the divorce?"

I swallowed hard. "I—I didn't say anything."

"Well, when you wrote to him, I mean."

"I never wrote to him."

Patsy straightened in surprise. "You mean you never told your dad how you felt? Not at all?"

"No way!" The sharpness in my voice echoed in the small room.

"Drew. *Why?*"

My insides trembled. Feeling strangely cold, I hugged my knees. "Well, I kept expecting *Dad* to call to talk about the divorce. But he never did. When he finally called months later, all he ever

134

asked about was the weather or school or some other stupid thing, so I decided that I'd never let on that I was disappointed. I didn't want Dad to know that he'd hurt me. Didn't want to give him the satisfaction.''

''I don't think knowing that would've made him very happy,'' Patsy said.

I shrugged.

''Besides,'' he went on, ''don't you think he deserved some kind of response? Even an angry one?''

''*No*. Not after what he did to us. Not after the *way* he did it to us. Patsy, my dad didn't *want* a response. He's a coward! He didn't love me enough to tell me in person. God, even a phone call would've been better than that—that—'' I gestured helplessly at the letter.

Patsy didn't say anything for a long time. ''I'm sorry, Drew,'' he said at last. ''I never would've guessed. I'm so sorry.''

''Don't be.'' I rested my cheek on my knees. I'd finally stopped trembling. ''It doesn't matter now. It's stopped hurting. I made it stop hurting. I don't care anymore. Not about the divorce. Not about Dad.''

''But if you don't care,'' Patsy said, ''then why keep the letter?''

My heart twisted. ''I don't know . . .''

Another silence. A bird chirped outside.

Patsy folded the letter and handed it to me. ''I don't know what to say. I can't believe he did it this way. There must be some kind of an explanation. You'd think he would've tried marriage counseling or something.''

I nodded. ''I know. Mom would've done any-

thing to keep herself and Dad together. She's like
that. Carries everything to the max. But Dad never
gave her the chance. Never told her what was
bothering him.''

"Maybe she never took the time to ask.''

My eyes blurred with tears. I thought back to
Jane's conversation with Dad. *"You never stood up
to her, never fought for what you wanted. And she
let you get away with it."*

Was there something more that Mom could've
done? Something more *I* could've done?

The small house seemed hot around me. Didn't
Patsy notice the heat? My head spun a little. Maybe
I needed some air. . . .

"Where are you going?'' Patsy asked, his eyes
drooping. The painkiller had started to take effect.

"I'm going to the store to get something for dinner. Why don't you sleep a little?'' I urged.

"Sure," he murmured. "Don't be gone too
long, okay?''

"I won't.''

I drove to the store and meandered up and down
the aisles, not thinking, not feeling. I felt safe going through the ordinary motions of shopping, of
choosing the fish, squeezing the fresh vegetables.
Every time a bit of my conversation with Patsy
came forward, I'd shove it back—back into a hot,
dark corner, back into the cobwebs.

By the time I reached the check-out counter, I
felt better. Hungry. Because of Patsy's accident, I'd
never eaten lunch. Maybe that's why I'd felt dizzy.
I drove back to Patsy's and hurried up the lawn to
his house, stooping to heft a large green coconut
from beneath a palm tree.

"Look what I found,'' I said, opening the door.

136

Patsy sat up, blinking. "What do you plan to do with that?"

"We can have it for dessert. I'm so hungry, I think I could gnaw off the husk."

"No, it isn't ripe yet. But we can get some juice out of it." Fully awake now, Patsy got up and took a huge cleaver from the kitchen. Out on the porch, he hacked off the top of the coconut.

"Looks like a hat," I said.

"Hmmm . . . that gives me an idea."

While I lit the charcoal for the hibachi and made a salad, Patsy used his pocket knife to carve a face on the husk, complete with toothy grin and impish eyes.

"Is that a tourist?" I asked, laughing.

"No." Patsy puffed out his chest and spoke in a deep voice: "No, silly woman. This Great Vacation God of Hawaii. He make sure you have happy summer—and don't burn dinner."

"Thank you for watching over us, O Great Vacation God," I intoned, bowing. Then I pointed to the couch. "Pats, you and your friend get back over there. You're supposed to rest, remember? I'm going to barbecue the fish now. Don't you move."

After dinner, Patsy played a few songs for me on his guitar. We sat on the couch together, watching the sunset colors melt into evening black. I lit a candle. Then Patsy put the guitar away and unplugged the phone.

"Come here," he said.

Being careful of the bandage on his forehead, we stretched out on the narrow couch, our arms around each other. We kissed for a long time. I felt breathless. Sometimes Patsy cupped my face in his fingers. Sometimes I'd brush his cheek with my eyelashes in little butterfly kisses. A languid warmth spread from my toes to my hair, until it felt as if Patsy and I were floating in the pool of moonlight that spilled through his window, the beams lapping at us, nudging us closer together. Patsy made a soft moan and moved slightly against me. I wanted to press even closer. I never wanted to stop kissing. . . .

Patsy lifted his face from mine. I gazed up into his eyes, smelling his skin, his suntan oil. Then I felt another pair of eyes watching me. I glanced over at the coffee table. The Great Vacation God grinned at us.

I giggled. "We're not alone."

"That's all right," Patsy said. "He makes a good chaperon."

I snuggled deeper into his arms. "This is so nice," I whispered.

"Mmmm." He yawned, then murmured: "It's getting late. Don't let me fall asleep."

"I won't."

When I woke up, the sky was just starting to get light.

Oh, *no.* I checked my watch. Six a.m.!

"Patsy, I've got to go home." I untwined myself, shaking my right arm, which had fallen asleep under him.

"Wh—what?" Patsy sat up. "What time is it?"

"Time for me to go. Come on, let me help you to bed."

Leaning against my shoulder, Patsy walked into the bedroom. He winced a little as he lay down. I covered him with a thin blanket. The morning air felt cool.

138

"Talk to you later," I whispered.

He mumbled something unintelligble. He was already falling back to sleep.

I tucked in my blouse, grabbed my pack, and started up the truck. It idled explosively in my ears against the early morning quiet. Maybe I could park it down the road a ways from home. I didn't want anyone to know how late—or rather, how early— I'd gotten back. If Dad and Jane had gone to bed at ten as usual, they'd never suspect. The front door was never locked. I could just tiptoe in.

I parked the truck. Started toward the house on foot—and froze. Dad was sitting on a lounge chair on the lanai. My heart sank. Why had he gotten up so early?

"Good morning," Dad said coldly. His mouth was set in a firm line. His eyes looked tired, pinched at the corners. And that's when I realized. Dad had never gone to bed. He had sat here all night, waiting. Waiting for me.

15

"Sit down, Drew," Dad ordered.

Without a word, I slung my pack to the grass and chose a chair on the opposite end of the lanai. My heart beat in funny jerks.

"Do you know what time it is?" Dad asked.

"Listen, let me explain. . . ."

"No, you listen." His finger jabbed the air. "We discussed your curfew the other night. You promised to be in on time or to call, if you would be late."

I crossed my arms. "I *did* call. Yesterday afternoon. Everybody knew I was at Patsy's. If you were so worried, why didn't you call his house?"

"We did. We couldn't get through."

"That's impossible. We were there all night." Then I remembered. Patsy had unplugged the phone.

I heaved a sigh. "Oh, I'm sorry, Dad. I blew it, all right? Is that what you want to hear? I didn't mean to spend the night there. We just fell asleep on the couch. I'm sorry. If you want to ground me, well, okay. Fine." I stood up to go.

"I'm not finished," Dad said. "Sit down."

140

I sat. There was something in his tone that hadn't given me a choice.

"It's more than just the curfew that concerns me," Dad said. He ran a hand through his hair, then leaned forward, arms resting on his knees. "It's Patsy. I know you like him, Drew. And I like him too. But I'm responsible for you while your mother's in Europe, and I think things are happening too fast between you."

I almost laughed. If he only knew I'd felt the same way!

"This is not funny," he insisted. "Sleeping with Patsy after only knowing him a week is hardly—"

I leapt up. "We didn't!" I cried. "I told you, we fell asleep, but nothing happened. *Nothing.*"

Dad continued as if he hadn't heard. "I don't want you to get hurt, Drew. You're only seventeen. So young. And Dillon's even younger. What do you suppose he'll think when he finds out his sister slept with—"

"But we *didn't.*" I towered over Dad, my fists clenched. "How can you do this? How can you talk about what Dillon thinks of *me?* What about your relationship with Jane? You two sleep together night after night, with Dillon right in the next room!"

Dad looked up at me. "Drew, please. That's different. Jane and I, we're older. We love each other. We have a commitment to each other. And we— we've decided to get married. Next weekend, before Kristin leaves."

I froze. My hands, stomach, and legs were a solid sheet of ice.

Dad and Jane. *Married.*

"I wanted to tell you differently, but—"

141

"How *were* you going to tell me?" I asked. "Was I going to get another letter, Dad? Or maybe find a scribbled note taped to the bathroom mirror? DEAR DREW, NICE WEATHER WE'RE HAVING. OH, BY THE WAY . . ." I laughed weakly. "How did you propose, Dad? Telegram? Carrier pigeon? Does Jane even *know* yet?"

"Oh, Drew," Dad whispered. "I'm sorry. I care about you so much. I just can't seem to tell you—"

"Send me a postcard." I scooped up my pack and started marching back down the drive. My stomach had knotted. Blood pounded in my ears.

"Drew, where are you going? Drew!"

I didn't answer. Just kept walking, my breath coming in gasps, gravel spraying under my feet. I'd had it. Had enough. There was no way now that I could stay at Dad's the rest of the summer. I'd have to go back home. Maybe stay with Kristin. But how could I leave Patsy? He'd think I was just trying to run away from him again. Well, I'd talk to him. After what I'd been through with Dad, he'd understand. He'd *have* to.

When I reached his house, the hot sun had just peeked over the hills. Quietly, I slid open the door. Patsy was still asleep, his face half-buried in a pillow. I kicked off my thongs and bent to kiss him on the ear.

"Drew?" he asked. He turned toward me and yawned. "Drew, what are you doing here?"

He looked so sleep-tousled, so boyish, it wrung my heart.

Patsy rubbed a hand across his eyes and sat up. He seemed to really see me for the first time.

142

"Drew, why did you come back? Has something happened? You look—what's wrong?"

"Nothing's wrong." I lay down, curled on my side, away from him. "Just had a little run-in with Dad, that's all. He's worried about us."

"Oh-oh. He read you the riot act about last night, didn't he? Look, it'll be okay. I'll call him later and explain everything."

"Don't bother. It won't change things between him and me. We're not ever going to get along. Better for all of us if I just leave."

Patsy was awake now. He turned me to face him. "You mean, go back to San Francisco?"

I could see the hurt in his eyes. I nodded.

"Oh, Drew." He reached out and took my hand. He stared down at it for a few minutes, as if gathering his thoughts.

"Drew," he repeated, "forget about us for a minute, okay? I'll be disappointed if you leave, but if you have to, you have to. I'll understand. But I don't understand why you won't try to work things out with your dad. Or at least tell him you're upset, that you're angry."

I pulled my hand away. "I told you before that I don't care anymore. And I'm not angry. I don't get angry."

"*Everybody* gets angry. But most people let it out. You just keep carrying it around with you."

"Now you sound like Jane."

"So what? Jane's done a lot of good for me. And you know I'm right, don't you? You're carrying this stuff around inside you, and it just keeps getting heavier and heavier. Aren't you tired of it, Drew? Aren't you?"

I didn't answer.

143

"Drew—"

"Yes," I finally whispered.

"Then *do* something about it! Scream or cry or throw things. I don't care. Do something. Anything!"

"I can't!" White-hot panic had welled up inside of me. I felt scared, as if someone had taken a sharp blade and slashed clean through my lifeline. I'd been cut off, set adrift to wash away, over the falls, down to the rocks below.

I got off the bed. Put on my thongs. Picked up my pack.

"Drew, you can't just leave." Patsy struggled out of bed. "We have to talk about this."

"I have to think," I said, slamming out of the house.

"Drew!" Patsy called. "Drew, please wait. I can't run after you. Drew, don't go!"

I didn't listen to his words. I started to run. Faster, my thongs slapping against my heels, against the asphalt. I had to keep running away from those edges, away from the cliffs.

I stopped, exhausted, when I reached Brennecke's. I sank down in the sand. I sat there for a long time, catching my breath, taking air in great gulps, trying to dispel the sick feeling still swirling in my head.

At last, I felt a little better. I looked around. The beach was deserted, except for one body-surfer. I watched him take a wave. With a kick of his flippers he flashed down the face of the turquoise wall, flying, his fist outstretched as if being pulled by some unknown force. Then, as my stomach lurched, as I knew the wave was going to lash

144

out and roll over him, there was another kick of flippers. The bodysurfer disappeared.

Startled, I sat up. The wave broke and rushed in. When the surf grew calm again, I could see the bodysurfer floating lazily toward another wave. He must have cut under and back. He'd escaped before the final moment, before he washed over the falls. He was safe. In control.

And then I understood.

Pasty was right. I *was* tired. Tired of being afraid. Tired of carrying the heavy weight of things I felt, things I needed to say. And that would never change. I would always be afraid of cliffs, tall buildings, airplanes . . . even the people I cared about. Unless *I* changed. Unless I was like that bodysurfer, coming right to the edge of a wave, facing that fear—and then cutting under and back to face myself. To face Dad . . .

Patsy met me at the door of his house.

"Drew," he said, sounding surprised and glad.

"I came back to apologize," I said. "I didn't mean to run off like that. Or to scare you or anything. I—just needed to be alone for a while."

"Come in."

I shook my head. "I can't stay. I have to go back to Dad's."

"To pack? . . . Or to talk?"

I smiled. "To talk."

Patsy sighed. "Will you come over later? Let me know how things go?"

"Of course. I came back now only because . . . because I wanted you to know where I was, so you wouldn't think I'd run out on you again."

145

Patsy nodded solemnly, acknowledging what that meant to him, and what it meant for us.

Then he smiled. "Hey, don't go yet, Drew. I have a little present for you." He pulled his sunglasses from the pocket of his shorts and slipped them onto my nose. "If you have problems facing your dad, just wear these. They hide a multitude of sins. Oh, and they're great for girl watching."

I laughed. "I'll remember that, Pats. See you later."

16

When I got back to the house, Dad, Jane, and Dillon were just coming out the door. Dad clenched the truck keys in his hand. He didn't see me standing at the edge of the lawn.

"Dillon, I want you to check the beach areas on foot," he instructed. "Jane, take the Subaru. Head to Koloa. She might be hitchhiking to the airport."

"What do you want me to do, Dr. Mueller?" Kristin called from the doorway.

"I want you to stay here, Kris, in case she comes back. She'll want to see someone she . . . likes. I'll check at Patsy's first, then head North to—" Dad's words broke off. He'd seen me now. They'd all seen me.

"Thank goodness," Jane said. The tip of her nose was red, as if she'd been crying.

"See? What'd I tell you?" Dillon proclaimed to the world at large. "I *told* you Druid wouldn't leave. I *knew* she wouldn't!"

Dad didn't say anything, but relief washed over his face. "Drew . . ." He spoke my name as if not quite believing it.

I shoved my hands into the pockets of my shorts.

"Hi," I said. It sounded inadequate, but I didn't know what else to say.

Dad's voice matched my own. "Drew, we were just about to search for you. We've been so worried. When you ran off, I was so afraid that . . . I didn't know—"

"I'm okay," I said. "And I'm sorry."

"No. I'm the one who's sorry."

I looked up and saw a sudden sadness glistening in Dad's eyes. I knew that look too well. I'd seen it when I'd left him standing alone in an airport, long ago. I'd seen it the day we moved from Santa Rosa back to the city. And I'd seen it every single time I had pushed him away with my words, with my hurt, during the last two weeks.

I swallowed at the lump in my throat.

Slowly, Dad closed the space between us. His arms eased around me, and he rested his chin on my head. My first reaction was to pull away. Then I pressed my face against his shirt, my arms around him, too.

"I'm so very, very sorry," he whispered.

I don't remember exactly when Jane slipped away. Or when Kristin dragged Dillon by the arm into the house. I don't remember how long Dad and I stood there. I just know that I was finally crying, the tears seeming to flow directly from my heart, like blood from an open wound. Dad rocked me back and forth, stroking my hair, saying my name over and over again, the rhythm of it soothing me, calming me.

I clung to him. I felt almost safe. Just like when I was a little girl and Dad could make things better without a word, with only a hug. But that wasn't enough now. It wasn't enough.

148

I'm not a little girl anymore, Dad, I thought. Maybe hugs and kisses and pats on the head worked when I was a kid, but not anymore. Being older is more complicated. Things have to be said, feelings explained, anger released—otherwise you can't grow. You can grow up. You can grow away. But you can never grow together: not as father and daughter, not as friend to friend. And especially not as individuals. Not until things are finally said and done . . .

I looked up at him. He cupped my cheek. "Dad," I said, my voice hoarse but firm. "Dad, we have to talk."

We sat underneath a tree in the soft grass. I pulled at the sweet petals of a plumeria. Dad sipped a mug of coffee. I knew he was nervous. He kept glancing at me and clearing his throat. This was so hard. For both of us.

"I really hated you," I began softly. "That letter—it made me feel lost. With you gone and Mom falling apart, there was nothing left. And I didn't understand. . . ."

"Things between your mom and me had been wrong for a long time," Dad said. "Yet I let it go on, without saying a word, hoping things would change. That *I* would change. Finally, I couldn't hope anymore. I had to pull away without warning. And I knew if I had to tell you, in person, about leaving, that I couldn't leave. And that was the wrong reason to stay."

"But, Dad." Tears started to my eyes again. "That letter, it hardly said anything."

"I know." Dad took my hand, then glanced away. "I was so afraid of saying the wrong thing.

149

Afraid of hurting you. Afraid of facing you. So I took the easy way out.''

"You told Mom you didn't love her anymore. That you'd just stopped.'' I almost whispered the words. It hurt to say them too loud. "I thought . . . I thought if you could stop loving her, you could stop loving me, too.''

Dad shook his head. "I don't think it's really possible to stop loving all at once. It happens gradually, without you even noticing. I stayed with your mom for years, even though I was unhappy, because I thought I loved her. But I was just loving how things were for us in the beginning. I was loving a memory. But that's not how it is with you, Drew. You're not a memory. You're here and now. I love you. I've never stopped.''

I closed my eyes. "I never really stopped, either. I just sort of forgot how to love you for a while.'' A pause. "Dad, I have so many things to say. About you and Mom. And Jane, too. Things that I'm not sure I like, but that I'll have to accept. But it's going to take some time to put it all together. And I don't know . . . I don't know if I can ever get it all out.''

"But we've got that time to work on it, don't we, Drew?''

I heard a note of desperation in his voice. And something else: love. That's when I knew for sure that I wouldn't be going home with Kristin.

I opened my eyes. "Sure, Dad,'' I said, smiling a little. "We've got the whole summer.''

Epilogue

I don't have to go, I tell myself. Pasty will understand. He knows about my fear: of heights, of cliffs, of falling. He'll let me turn away, scrambling back up the rocks to the road. But if I turn back, he'll go on without me. And I don't want to let go of his hand.

Carefully, we make our way down to a ledge above the sea. The waves hurtle against the rocks, spray thrashing white and high, almost sucking at our feet, trying to drag us down and out and away. . . .

In his hand, Patsy holds the coconut: the Great Vacation God, with grinning mouth and impish eyes.

"Time to make the sacrifice," Patsy says solemnly, but his lips twitch with laughter. Inside the husk he places a sliver of surf wax, a plumeria, and, at the last minute, his sunglasses.

"Why?" I ask, surprised.

He only smiles. "Your turn."

I take the coconut in my hands. From the pocket of my shorts I pull out a crumpled envelope. It contains a single sheet of cream-colored paper. A

151

letter with neat, angular script and a hotel logo embossed in one corner. Without thinking, I shove the letter into the husk, then clap on the top.

I feel a sudden surge of freedom. "To a great summer!" I cry, and fling the coconut into the blue. The water devours it. Then a wave rises up, speeding toward the rocks. Patsy moves back.

"Look out, Drew!" he calls. "Get away from the edge!"

But I don't have to. Not anymore. I know there will always be edges to fear. But I won't fall. I can stand firm now. I'm in control.

The swell crashes against the rocks. It tugs at the toes of my tennis shoes, spraying me, drenching me, and then recedes. Water drips off my nose. Then, wet and laughing, I turn away from the edge and take Patsy's outstretched hand.

LEE WARDLAW is the author of more than a dozen books for children and young adults, including *Corey's Fire*, a 1991 Children's Choice book.

Not overly fond of flying, Lee does manage to make the trip to Kauai almost every year, where she enjoys body-surfing, exploring, and moonlit walks on the beach with her husband, Craig.

A former teacher, Lee now writes full-time from her home office in Santa Barbara, California.